CW00522111

The
Unlicensed
Magician

The Unlicensed Magician

KELLY
BARNHILL

2015

ISBN
978-1-84863-919-5 (Signed Edition)
978-1-84863-918-8

Design and layout by Alligator Tree Graphics.
Printed in England by T. J. International.

PS Publishing Ltd / Grosvenor House /
1 New Road / Hornsea, HU18 1PG / England

editor@pspublishing.co.uk / www.pspublishing.co.uk

NOW

THE VOX SPUTTERS TO LIFE, ON SCHEDULE, AT FOUR A.M.

Even the chickens are asleep.

"CITIZENS!" it shouts, "ROUSE YOURSELVES! THROW OFF YOUR BEDCLOTHES! PREPARE FOR A MESSAGE FROM THE MINISTER HIMSELF. TODAY, BELOVED CITIZENS, IS A GLORIOUS ONE. RUB YOUR EYES! CLEAR YOUR THROATS! THE ANTHEM IS AT HAND!"

Every citizen has a Vox. It's the law. Everyone knows the schedule. Still, the jangly arrival of the announcer's voice is a jolt in the nation-wide quiet. In households across the country, traitorous pillows cover otherwise patriotic ears, and in the darkness, thousands of children feel their inconstant eyes well up, mourning the loss of yet another night's rest.

Just outside the farmhouse, listening to the panicked squeal of the Vox, the junk man's daughter stares up at the scattered stars, and the harsh glint of planets cutting into the black. The hay under her back has clumped and matted over the course of the night, and everything is damp.

Her father—well, her foster-father—is lying on top of the heap of gathered treasures, head below hips, arms splayed over cracked urns and dead radios, skinny legs hanging over the side in unlikely angles. He snores prodigiously, and even from where she lies, a few yards off, she can smell the decaying drunkenness; her eyes burn from the alcoholic cloud emanating from his mouth and off-gassing from his skin.

He calls it whiskey, but it is not whiskey. It is a homemade alcohol that he brews in a boot, and distils in small batches using a miniature coil that he designed himself.

His daughter is amazed that he hasn't gone blind, or blown his hands off. She knows that it has something to do with the unintentional protection that she affords him simply by existing, which doesn't help her situation.

What will happen if she is discovered? How will he survive without her? Who will take care of him if she is gone?

(Not *if*, her heart knows. *When.*)

The junk man groans in his cart.

"Did you say something, my Sparrow?" he slurs.

"No, Papa," she says. "Go back to sleep." By the time she finishes the word "papa", he is already snoring. Still she says it. "Papa". Her voice is like the clasp of fingers curling around a living heart and holding on for dear life.

The anthem blares—a long, plodding, minor-key affair, like a funeral dirge. It is sung this time by two old men, their voices tired and sagging.

Former generals, the girl knows without trying, *and today is their last day.*

Being a general is a risky business, after all. Little failures are more likely to catch the Minister's eye, and no one wants to catch the Minister's eye; not if he wants to keep his own head. The two men heave a great sigh the moment the song ends. One begins to sob.

"Do you see, beloved citizens, how patriotism stirs the hearts of even the most hardened of men? Let us all take a moment to wipe our own flowing tears! Let us all pause to blow our leaking noses!"

The Vox devolves into a chorus of fake sobbing. Someone makes a honking sound like a dying goose, or a broken horn.

The junk man's daughter sighs. She pulls herself to her feet, wraps what used to be a boiled-wool blanket but is now little more than a scrap, around her shoulders and tiptoes, barefoot, across the frost-kissed lawn to the window of the farmhouse. She shivers, but not from the cold. The inhabitants do not know that she spent the night on their lawn with her beyond-drunk father. Even if they looked out the window, they would see *him* and they would see the cart, but they wouldn't see *her*. Most likely, they wouldn't.

Hardly anyone can see the junk man's daughter. Those who can do so, she can count on one hand. Others can see her from time to time, but without any regularity (and most don't like her much, when they do. She is the junk man's daughter, after all; tainted, clearly, by his drinking and shiftlessness.) It is lonely, this invisibility. Of course it is lonely. But safe. *Safe.*

But for how long, she finds herself wondering more and more lately, *and for what purpose?* Even now, having lived this way for fifteen years, she still has no idea.

She leans her chin on the sill and rests her forehead against the glass. She can feel the vibrations of the Vox's voice buzzing in her skull.

"Beloved citizens! Has there ever been so great a nation?" the Vox chuckles at the very thought of it. "Now, gather close. We have items of business to discuss before our dear minister comes to bring you his message of hope and peace."

The farmhouse inhabitants have ignored the Vox, and have kept their lights off and bedroom doors closed. Likely, they have fashioned earplugs for this very purpose (these cannot be bought, of course. Earplugs are illegal. Ignoring the Vox is also illegal. This family, like many this far away from the Capitol, sometimes lives by their own rules. For now, anyway. The junk man's daughter finds this charming).

The Vox drones on for a bit—new regulations for the sale of homemade baked goods. New regulations for the admission of young children into Obedience School (there is, the Vox assures the people, no place in This Great Nation for disobedient toddlers. All children over twelve months of age must now report to Obedience School. No exceptions. Starting today.). New regulations for the sale of liquor (the punishment for unlicensed sales is no longer life in prison, but is now, as it should be, death. A righteous and glorious decision. All hail the Minister).

The farmhouse is warm and cosy. Hand-stitched crazy quilts draping over the sagging sofa and rough-hewn chairs. A wide, hand-planked wooden table with a bowl of field flowers in the centre.

There are five people who live in this house—two parents and three boys. The youngest, not quite eleven, still attends Obedience School. The older boys are thirteen and seventeen, and they both work the farm.

The junk man's daughter knows this family well. She has sat with them at their dinner table as they ate. She has listened at the foot of the boys' shared bed as their mother or father took turns snuggling in and reading the stories from ancient copies of illegal books. She has peered over the mother's shoulder as she worked through the mathematics of farming, weeping as the numbers didn't add up. She has lain on the floor while they made music in the living room with homemade instruments. They never see her. They have no idea.

The oldest boy, Jonah, has taken to building contraband telescopes in the backyard. The junk man's daughter has stood near him as he peered into the sky in the darkest hours of the night, her breath clouding before her face like ghosts. She has listened as he muttered to himself—rattling names that she has never heard— Anteres, Canis Majoris, Andromeda. There are books with numbers and diagrams in the house. Old things, carefully rebound; remnants from another world. The family regards them as precious.

She has peered over his shoulder. She has watched him fuss over his own charts. She has listened to his whispery voice. He never saw her.

And yet…

He wears a locket around his neck. He doesn't know where it came from; he wears it anyway. She has watched him wrap his fingers around the locket and hang on tight. She has noticed how their breathing in and their breathing out becomes synchronised. Moments when he speaks into the darkness: a question, always. And moments when she almost answers back.

But there is no Jonah this morning, and no Isaac and no Benjamin. There is only the voice of the Vox, and its announcer's excitement reaching a fever pitch.

"Can you turn that thing down, my Sparrow?" the junk man slurs, though she can tell that he is still dreaming. No one can turn down a Vox, and dismantling them sets off an alarm.

Whole families have disappeared following Vox-infractions.

"I've already done it, Papa," she says. "*Sleep.*" Her voice, heavily laden with intention does what she hopes it would do; the junk man sinks into unconsciousness. He will not rouse before noon.

"HE IS HERE, CITIZENS!" the announcer nearly screeches. His voice is hoarse. He trembles and panics. "THE MINISTER IS HERE! ALL HAIL THE MINISTER!"

The junk man's daughter, the Sparrow, the child that never lived, the guttersnipe, the tramp, the trash-spawn, the dirty thief, the tart-in-training, and every other name that has been assigned to her in

5

her young life, presses her hands against the glass. The family may notice her fingerprints. She hopes they do.

The Vox scrambles a bit, static scratching the quiet world. The Minister has no magic, of course, but he has spent enough of his overly extended life in the presence of magic, and it interferes with radio signals. His voice stutters and halts. It is far away. It is in a cloud.

The girl holds her breath.

"Are you listening?" the Minister says through the Vox. His voice is tender, loving, stern; and underneath it all, terribly, terribly afraid.

The junk man's daughter nods.

The Minister clears his throat. "It has come to my attention, my beloved children, that…" His voice trails off. He clucks his tongue. Even his bodiless voice seems to shake its head. "Well. It seems so crazy to say it out loud."

A bugle, very far away, plays the Anthem. Its long, sad notes slide under the Minister's voice.

"Have I not loved you, my children? Have I not cared for you? Have I not kept your bellies full and your wounds healed and your homes safe from harm?"

His voice, she can hear, is amplified, not by the radio, but by magic. Whose magic, she has no idea. The last remnants from the depleted magic children—dying now, if they aren't dead already. The Sparrow shivers, thinking of them.

"But nonetheless, I have heard reports of…*oddness*. Here and there. Things that *have no right to be happening*. It is astonishing to me that there could be, somewhere in this nation, an unlicensed magician. Laughable, even. It is beyond ludicrous to believe that such a level of *flagrant rule-breaking* could exist here, in this *most blessed nation*."

The Sparrow's heart gives a little thrill. She presses her lips lightly against the glass. Gives it a kiss. The house shivers.

"And yet, the facts prove otherwise. An unlicensed magician now walks among us. But not for long. Not if we can help it. You and me together."

His voice trembles. He worries. He yearns. He fears. He is beside himself. The girl is moved with compassion.

"To you, my beloved citizens, I say this: *watch; observe; report.* Even small things. I am relying on you."

She loves the house. She loves the family. She loves the Minister, too. She is suffocating from so much love. Her very skin is stretched tight with it, like a balloon about to burst.

"And to you—*little magician*," his breath rattles. There is a hiss in his voice; he is afraid. She can feel his fear in her very skin.

Poor baby, she thinks.

"You have no name."

I have a name, she thinks. *My mother whispered it before I was born. And then she forgot it. I am the only one who knows my name.*

"You have no place. You are lost. You are a lost lamb in a dark, cruel wood."

No, she thinks, *it is you who is lost.*

"But I am coming."

I am waiting for you.

"I will find you, my darling," the Minister says.

I will lead you to me, as a spider leads a fly.

"I will catch you. I will claim you. I will love you to bits."

As I love you, the junk man's daughter thinks, *as I love you, and love you, and love you.* And she does; she loves him *so much*, as she loves everyone. It is dangerous, this love, and she can't control it. It is ever so much bigger than she, and growing by the day. It is a river, an ocean. The sky. Her love crushes planets, shatters suns, burns whole galaxies to cinders and dust.

"And then, child, I will drain you."

Yes, she thinks, *you can try.*

7

"Do you hear me? I WILL DRAIN YOU DRY."

Try, she thinks, *try and you will drown in it. You will drown, and drown, and drown.*

And for the first time, she knows it is true.

2

THEN

THE FIRST APPEARANCE OF THE BORO COMET, AND THE subsequent appearance of magic children, occurred shortly after the Minister first began his long and fruitful rule.

No one can say how long ago—how very, very long ago—this was.

Only the Minister knows, and he won't say.

The comet simply appeared one day in the eastern skies, fat and shining like a pendant on the neck of the horizon. Astonished astronomers clamoured over one another, elbowing their colleagues out of the way in an effort to be the first one to name it. In the end, it was named in honour of the Minister's father—a dear man who had met an unfortunate and untimely end a decade earlier in a tragic firing-squad accident (all condolences to the Minister). No one knew at the time—aside from the comet's mysterious and surprising appearance—the impact the object would have on them all.

No one knew that the whole world was about to change.

First, it was the dreams, crowding thick and fast, night after night, into the slumbering skulls of the populace. No one mentioned it, but everyone knew; every man, woman and child was marked by pale faces and darkened eyes and mouths slack from dreaming. And *oh*! What dreams!

Then, shortly after the comet disappeared, the babies arrived—one hundred and two of them, in counties all around the nation. Magic babies.

They all had, to a one, a curious birthmark curling out of their navels—a strange spiral that glowed in the dark. They were volatile, some of them, liable to make doors explode, syringes vanish, or catapult their mothers from one side of the room to the other. There were broken bones, cracked teeth, annoyed nurses.

Other babies were more benign, liable to make their teddy bears sentient so as to see to the important work of infant cuddling when their busy families could not. Or, they made lullabies come gurgling out of bed sheets and cradles. Some endowed their panicked fathers with new, round breasts, laden with milk. Others, remarkably, grew wings.

The Minister, thinking fast, had the children rounded up and sequestered for study.

"They could be dangerous," the Minister explained. "They could be sick," he went on, "or contagious."

He paid the families, of course. Handsomely. So they were in no position to argue. Plus, he had all the guns.

"So many things," the Minister mused, "can be accomplished with guns. How many more things might be accomplished with magic?"

And so his experiments began.

He used earplugs to drown out the screams.

3

NOW

THERE ARE SIGNS ALL OVER THE MARKETPLACE.

UNLICENSED PRACTICES OF MAGIC ARE PROHIBITED BY LAW.
BE A MODEL CITIZEN.
WATCH.
LISTEN.
REPORT.
FAILURE TO REPORT
IS A FAILURE TO YOUR COUNTRY.
FAILURE IS NOT TOLERATED.

The signs appeared the night before, sometime after midnight. No one knows who hung them. The people in the marketplace are doing their best not to notice the signs. Their eyes slide from side to side. They talk about the weather. They talk about their children's need for new shoes. They talk about their recent teeth extractions. Why would they mention the signs? They have done nothing wrong.

They are not breaking the law. They say this over and over, in the silences of their hearts, until it feels true.

The junk man does not have a stall, and pays no tax to the Mayor—never has. The Mayor never forced the issue, and if he did, the junk man would simply sell elsewhere, and then the populace would revolt, and then there would be a new Mayor—after both tarring and feathering the first. Or reporting him to the Minister.

It's tricky work, being the Mayor. Times being what they are.

It snowed the day before, but now the winds have slowed and the sky has cleared, and the day is fine and warm, with the easing dampness of a world still soft, but readying itself for a freeze.

The junk man's daughter eats an apple. She sits on the edge of the cart while the junk man stands off to the side, conferring with a matron in low, hushed tones.

"As you can see," the junk man says, pulling an apple out of the empty bowl, and holding it with a flourish on his open palm. He tosses it without looking at his daughter, who plucks it from its high, clean arc, and places it with the rest of the apples on her apron. Each apple came from the empty bowl. "It's just a bowl. Lovely, yes? A couple of chips, sure, but the ceramic is of good quality and you don't find that kind of glaze work nowadays." The matron watches as he reaches in. The bowl is empty. Anyone can see it is empty. He pulls another apple from the empty bowl. This one he brings to his mouth, and bites. The skin is red and firm and the flesh is a creamy white. A burst of sweet apple smell hangs between the two of them like a cloud. He grins.

"Delicious. Would you like one?"

The matron nods slowly, her eyes wide.

"Well, help yourself." He winks.

Slowly, she reaches in. She moves as though she is dreaming. The bowl is empty. Her fingers find an apple—this one golden in colour.

She bites. It tastes like honey—the junk man's daughter can tell just by looking at it. The matron closes her eyes, and her lips spread across the crushed apple in a smile.

"How much?" the matron says, with her mouth full.

It takes fifteen minutes to negotiate a price. The junk man's daughter tires of the conversation and returns her gaze to the marketplace. There is a toad on her lap, and two identical chickens pecking the ground at her feet. The toad settles itself in the folds of her skirt. She caresses its head absently.

The matron leaves with the bowl balanced on her hip, pulling apple after apple from its empty depths and shoving them into her pockets. The girl shakes her head. It was a mistake, that bowl. Like so many others. Her eyes slide back over to the signs.

She doesn't want anyone to get into trouble. She never has.

The junk man waves as the matron disappears and counts his earnings, dropping each coin into his purse with a pleasant jingle.

"Oh, my Sparrow, my Sparrow, my Sparrow!" he croons at his daughter, "And oh, the cleverness of me!" he enthuses, throwing his arms wide open. He wobbles and giggles and gives a little hiccup.

"You stole that line," the girl says, though it isn't exactly true. The junk man cannot read very well, and even if he could, he would never have encountered such a turn of phrase in a book. Only the books that the Minister has approved exist anywhere in the country, and the Minister doesn't approve of much.

Still, there is much that is suddenly available to the junk man when his daughter is nearby. Images pop into his head; proverbs, quotes, even a song or two, and worlds and worlds of stories. He collects them the way he collects his junk, which is to say, *joyfully*.

His daughter gives him a snort. "And anyway, you are not that clever, Papa."

He gives her a bow and blows her a kiss, and it nearly breaks her in two. It is a good life they have, the two of them. It will kill her to leave it behind. She doesn't know why, but she knows a change is coming. She can feel it hover, just out of reach, like the sureness of a coming storm.

The church pastor wanders over, his steps weighted and slow. Sweaty skin, hooded eyes, and a red, red nose.

"Ah," the junk man says, "Reverend. Do I have the perfect thing for you." He ambles toward the half-drunk pastor, all bony knees and elbows. He is barbed wire and braided grass holding up a patched suit. He gives the pastor a foxy grin and a conspiratorial wink and shows him a bottle that, as far as he can tell, will never run dry.

The Sparrow shakes her head and turns away. She cups her hands and ladles the toad onto the ground between the identical chickens, first giving the top of its head a quick kiss. The toad bellows indignantly—not for the kiss, but for the separation from the girl. He loves that girl, desperately. So do the chickens, and she loves them back.

She slides into the crowd. There are people who can see her today—unusual, though it's been happening more and more lately, and it's not always pleasant. An old man tips his hat and then puckers his lips at her.

"Oh come now, guttersnipe," he says. "One kiss."

She shakes her head and darts away. She bumps into an old woman with a basketful of muffins for sale.

"Hmph," the woman says. "Watch where you're bumping, little tramp," she hisses, picking up the muffins and brushing the grit off with her fingers, checking this way and that to make sure no potential customers noticed. "Off with you now. Shoo!"

The woman doesn't notice that the number of muffins in the basket has inexplicably doubled. She will only realise that something was wrong much later, when she will count her earnings at the end of the day and realise that her purse is nearly twice as full as it was supposed to be. She will have no explanation for it. None at all.

She will not remember the girl.

The Sparrow tries to buy meat from the butcher with the coins she lifted from the junk man's purse. The butcher gives her a poisonous glare.

"Oh," he says, throwing his hands up, "you're paying me this time, are you? Well, maybe we should throw a party."

She presses her lips together and says nothing. He's not lying. She *has* stolen from him. She's surprised he knows. Sucking her lips between her teeth and biting down hard, she points at a good-looking bit of salt pork, which he wraps for her begrudgingly.

I'm sorry, she wants to say. But she doesn't.

He has a wound on his shoulder. It is wrapped, but the wrappings are soaked with a yellow fluid, and red streaks seep across his skin. He is sweaty and shivering.

The Sparrow tilts her head to the left. *Yellow,* she thinks. *Yellow, yellow, yellow.*

The red streaks start to shrink.

"Thank you," she says when he hands her the meat, and she hands him the money. "Thank you for everything."

She slips back into the crowd and disappears.

Well, the butcher thinks, *she didn't disappear. I just suddenly wasn't able to see her. With all the people, she was sucked into the crowd.*

Except that's not exactly what happened. She wasn't moving, and the crowd didn't suck her anywhere. She simply vanished.

Wait, the butcher thinks, *what am I saying? Who vanished? I haven't seen anyone all day.* He shakes his head. He has no memory of the junk man's daughter. He stares at the coins in his hand, confusion clouding his face. Even more confusing, the wound on his shoulder has begun to itch. He is crazed with itching. He throws off the bandages, and realises that his wound is gone, and his skin is whole. There is nothing that shows where the injury was. His skin is hale and firm, and smooth as a baby's.

Even stranger, on the spot where the wound once was: a coin. A big, gold coin.

Yellow, the butcher thinks. *Yellow, yellow, yellow.*

The junk man's daughter watches from twenty feet away. She hadn't moved. The butcher simply doesn't see her. She shrugs and continues on her way.

She stops at the cheese maker's, and the bread smith's and the beekeeper's, buying enough to keep her father fed and whole. The marketplace is crowded today—it's harvest time, and everyone's yields are impressively high this year. The beekeeper's stall is crowded with jars, and she sells honeycombs by the barrel. The pigs are fatter, the milk has twice the cream, and the potatoes are as big as boulders.

It will all go away, unfortunately. The rest of the nation is in a food shortage. This Province has been the only one oddly blessed with abundance, which means that soon it will all be gathered, crated, and shipped away.

There is a frenzy of buying, people getting what they can afford before…

"Sparrow!"

The girl looks up and sees Marla, the egg woman—all broad shoulders and wide hips and ferocious biceps—tossing her neighbours out of the way as she hurries across the square.

Marla has loved the Sparrow for as long as she could remember, and the Sparrow loves her back.

"Marla," the girl says with the beginnings of a smile—one that fades the moment she sees the look on Marla's face.

"Run, child," the egg woman says. "Soldiers. The soldiers are back."

She throws out her arms, blocking the girl from view; as though all that was needed to keep the girl from harm was the formidable presence of her own body.

"But my father—"

"I'll see to him. The constable is distracting the soldiers. He won't let anything happen to you. None of us will. Run, child. Run now."

The egg woman turns and walks toward the soldiers, strong as a tank. She has a basket of homemade cheeses hooked in the crook of her arm. She has a basket of astonishingly fine eggs from her battalions of Most Remarkable Hens. Indeed, there are no hens quite like them, thanks to her little Sparrow.

She'll use them if she has to.

The Sparrow hesitates. She looks to the green grocer and the cobbler. She looks to the berry man and the candle maker. No one sees her. The soldiers stand on the far side of the square, their electronic eyes focussed on the eggs in the basket.

"Whips up like none other," the egg woman says loudly. "Thick as cream." They also cure acne, heal burns, mend shoes, seal cracks and make meringues that will melt in the mouth. (They can also, in a pinch, secure a lover for the night. Very powerful, these eggs. Not magic, though. Surely not.)

The Sparrow calls for her father. She calls for the constable. She calls for the egg woman. No one comes. She wobbles, she flickers, and she flies away.

Later, people will say that they saw a flash of a patched apron catch a breeze and fly above the heads of the crowd.

"No," someone will counter, "it wasn't an apron. It was feathers."

"Not feathers," someone else will say, "wings. Patchwork wings."

"Hogwash," a third will swear. "It was a flock of sparrows. Sparrows and sparrows and sparrows. And then they were gone."

4

THEN

THE SPARROW COULDN'T REMEMBER BEING BORN.

She *could* remember, however, parts of her life within the watery womb of her mother. She could remember the sound of her mother's worry. She could remember the soothe of her father's voice, and then the bite of her father's rage, and the silence he left behind.

She remembered the Boro Comet, though she could not see it. She remembered it like a flash in the dark, and the surge of...*something*...coming up from under her like a wave.

Then she was something *else*. Even then, she knew. She knew her hands, she knew her mouth, she knew her toes, and she knew her magic. She knew these things without the power of names.

She heard the fear in her mother's voice at the mention of *Boro Comet*. But it wasn't the comet that made her like this.

It wasn't the flash that changed her, it was the wave. The wave from underneath. The Boro Comet doesn't *make*: it *draws*. She knows it in her bones.

5

NOW

Every Vox in the nation sputters to life at once.

"Citizens," it screeches, "your cooperation has been noted. Your minister asked and your minister has received. Long live the minister. Thousands of patriots flooded our message lines, our video centres and our offices. So many beautiful accusations. So many justifiable concerns. They will be rewarded—men, women and children all. They will be rewarded."

A crackle.

A breath.

A beat.

"And for those of you who know and do not tell...."

Another breath, and another. The Vox is silent. Until...

"Oh citizens," the Vox whispers. "Oh, my precious citizens. *I cannot, cannot say.*"

6

THEN

THE MINISTER HAD NEVER COUNTED ON THE WIND. HE BUILT his tower higher and higher—a wobbly, twisty, unlikely-looking structure, uncurling like seaweed toward the shimmering limit of the sky. Dark stones, blackened windows; impossible without magic, without his little magicians.

He loved them.

He couldn't bear to think of them.

He shoved them out of his mind.

Look! His tower! It is a marvel. It was higher than any structure in the history of the world. The Minister knew the history of the world; he had all the history books, after all. The ones he hadn't burned, anyway, and while the books told of impressive structures, they never mentioned the winds.

The wind, at the top of the tower, nearly sent him careening to his death, which would have been unfortunate seeing how long—how very long—he had spared himself the unpleasantness of dying. Falling off his own tower? Certainly not. He started binding himself with straps to keep him in place as he gazed at the sky through his stargazer, and watched for the first glimpse of the Boro Comet.

Four times a century it came. The Minister had seen it more times than he could count, and now he would see it pass by once again—*and so close*—but he still would not be able to catch it. Not yet, anyway. How many more magic children would he need until his tower was tall enough? Ten? Hundreds? Thousands? How many enhancements would he need before he could pluck the comet from the sky and carry it in his pocket forever?

It sickened him, of course, this business with the children, but the sickness in his heart didn't interfere with the surety of his will. Besides, the first, singular act of cruelty made the thousands that followed infinitely easier.

He needed that comet. He needed it desperately. It was all he could think about.

There were large red flowers growing along the edges of the walls defining the rooftop patio—a gift from one of his magic children, right before she died.

"To help you breathe," she had said kindly, before she breathed her last. Her lips were pale, her eyes were the colour of milk, her hair had fallen out months before. He usually did not learn the names of his magic children—or anyone, really. People die so quickly when they are not enhanced, and only the Minister is enhanced; he has seen to that. But the magic children, they die quicker. Best not to know them.

This one, though, this one he knew. Not her name, of course, just the *fact* of her—that inscrutable bit of the Self that cannot be drawn or recorded or named, and after all these years, he still mourned her; a raw, painful, immediate feeling of loss.

Red flowers, his heart whispered. *Red, red, red, red.*

He picked a flower, breathed deeply, and felt a tightening in his throat. He inserted the flower stem into his lapel and returned his gaze to the stars.

"Soon," he said, waiting for the first glimmer of the comet to come into view. "Soon," and he shivered, thinking of the coming magic, blessing the land. Thinking of the women with bellies about to swell with children imbued with the power to assist their Minister. Living only for him until they died.

"Soon," he said, and he imagined himself plucking the comet from the sky as though it was a candied fruit at the top of a large, luminous pastry. A delight meant for him, and him alone.

He fell asleep at the top of his tower, wrapped in wind, as the taste of sweetness and magic and promise lingered on his tongue.

7

NOW

THE BOY NAMED JONAH MAKES HIS WAY TO THE EGG WOMAN'S house. Very few people know the way. Indeed, Marla the egg woman can count those who know on one hand, and Jonah is not one of them.

She removes the small pistol she keeps in her ample brassiere and points it at the boy.

"Give me three reasons why I shouldn't shoot you, son," she says this casually, as though asking his opinion on whether bulbs should be planted in September or October. The gun in her hand is small and bright. She holds it perfectly still.

The boy puts up one hand. The other grips a locket around his neck. "I…"

"I can give you one why I *should*." A mild smile, a narrowed eye. "Trespassing."

"I…"

She rolls her eyes. "Really? That's the best you can do?"

"I'm sorry, Miss," the boy says. "I truly don't know what brought me here. I…" He shakes his head as though to dislodge sleep from his brain. "I'm not sure *what* brought me here. I've certainly never been here before."

Marla gives a sidelong glance to her right. She shakes her head with a harrumph. "You're Laney Tice's oldest boy, yes?"

He nods.

"Your mother's a good woman. A clear mind in a sea of pudding-heads. She'd miss you if you didn't come home." She sets the gun back in her lap. "Greet her for me, will you?"

He nods again. His face is muddled, darting eyes in a tangled brow.

"Well," she says firmly, "off you go."

"Yes," Jonah says, "off I go." He is about to say something more. His voice catches and he says nothing. He turns, takes two steps away, and then freezes.

Marla groans.

He spins around. "Scorpio," he nearly shouts.

"What's that, child?"

"Orion's belt."

Marla sighs and shakes her head. "Jonah Tice, what are you on about?"

"Delphinius and Draco, and Cassiopeia. Polaris. The arm of the Milky Way." He closes his eyes and presses his hands to his face. "I came here with a girl. I've seen her before."

Marla feels her stomach drop and her mouth go dry. "Now," she rasps, "that's enough of this silliness."

The boy's face is light and glowing. He holds his hands open before him, as though wanting to catch something that he has lost; as though it might fall from the sky. "She wore no shoes."

"It's cold." There is the acidic bite of panic in her throat. "No one goes barefoot in this weather. You imagined it."

"She wore a dress made of scraps and a coat that was too big, and a face made out of sky." His breath comes in quick gasps.

24

He loves her, Marla thinks, her skin going cold.

"Now that's just foolishness." She tries to scoff. It is a thin, brittle sound.

"Sparrow," the boy whispers.

"*No.*" *Shut your mouth,* she thinks. Her heart screams it. *Shut your stupid mouth.*

"Sparrow." The boy's face falls into itself, like a sleeper waking up.

"A trick of the light," she says. "I mean an active imagination. I think you should go."

"Sparrow," he says with more insistence, as though it is the most important word in the world.

Marla points her pistol at the ground to the left of the boy's feet and pulls the trigger. He yelps. "Get out." Her voice is dead calm. Her face is a stone. She shoots again, this time on his right side, and slightly closer.

He turns and runs as though pursued by wolves.

"Don't come back, or I'll sic my dogs on you." This, of course, is an empty threat. Years ago, maybe, her dogs could have torn the poor child limb from limb, but not anymore. They are impossibly old, plus they are drunk. Drunk in love with the Sparrow.

The Sparrow sits on Marla's right, leaning her head on the older woman's muscular shoulders. She has not just arrived. She has been there the whole time.

"I told you," the girl says.

"This proves nothing. The boy is nothing but a bundle of junk and sighs, juicy thoughts and sweaty socks. It's not magic what drew him; it's pheromones. I knew boys would be sniffing around in your vicinity some day, so it's no surprise. Pay him no mind. He's the first of many."

"Don't be mean," the Sparrow says. "He's nice."

"God," Marla snorts, "please."

"I must go find Papa." She stands and kisses Marla on the top of her head.

"I wish you didn't have to go," Marla says. "And don't follow that boy home."

"I won't," the girl lies.

She disappears down the trail.

"Don't go," Marla whispers to no one in particular. "Please."

8

THEN

THE BORO COMET APPEARED IN THE SKY FOUR TIMES A CENTURY, which meant that four times a century pregnant women in his country would fuss and worry over the possibility of bearing a child with magic, and four times a century the government sent operatives into the hospitals and clinics.

They listened to rumours, hired spies and tattletales, and read furtive glances. They measured the middles of women of childbearing age. They banned prophylactics. They made lists of the names of pregnant women and their due dates. No one knew how many children would be born marked by magic—it was different every time—but the papers were ready and the payouts accounted for.

The nation's women did their best to protect themselves. They made their husbands sleep in the yards, outhouses and sheds. They researched herbs to promote impotency and snuck them into the sandwiches of the men they knew. They developed headaches. Those who found themselves pregnant anyway drew runes on their doorways and draped white sashes over their bellies. They prayed and prayed for unmarked babies.

27

Not a magic child, they whispered, *please not a magic child.*

They were, after all, *expensive* children, full of heartbreak and loss. They were taken, worked, depleted, and died young. This was well known. They were children who belonged not to their families, but to the government, and no one wanted to bear a government child.

The Sparrow was conceived under the spell of the Boro. Two months before she was born, her mother had been rounded up with the other pregnant women and held in a high-security maternity ward, with nurses trained in martial arts and doctors who were excellent marksmen.

Even the orderlies had military training.

"No security measure is too great when it comes to protecting these precious mothers and their blessed progeny," the Minister intoned on the Vox.

They had stylists on staff to coif the hair of the expectant mothers, aestheticians to de-clog their pores, manicurists to see to their quick-bitten nails. They were given the best food, the sweetest drinks, and the highest-quality drug cocktails to imbue them with a giddy sense of well-being. The mothers felt as though they were floating through clouds of feathers and bubbles. They forgot about their families, about their bellies, about everything. They were happier than they had ever been in their lives.

The Minister congratulated himself heartily.

"A regular humanitarian," he said to no one in particular.

The Sparrow's mother couldn't get enough of it. She stole drug patches from the haunches of passed-out mothers in the recreation hall, or in the bathroom, or the morgue. She raided the trashcans, licked them clean.

The Sparrow, in her unborn watery world, was as addled as her mother. She dreamed of a tower as high as the sky. She dreamed of a jewel hovering over the world, pulling energy toward itself like a magnet, or a black hole. She dreamed of a wave pulling out of the centre of the world, of a man riding its crest, a look of ecstasy on his face. She dreamed of a wobbly tower, a wobbly cart and red flowers, yellow coins and of a girl disappearing into the sky.

She dreamed of her mother, and then there was only darkness.

9

NOW

No one sees the junk man's daughter. Not today, or at least not so far.

She wears a dress that she made herself from cast-off bits of fabric and a man's belt, wound twice around her waist, and a large, wool jacket that used to belong to the junk man, but now belongs to her, in theory. She has nothing on her tiny feet. Her soles are black and thick with dust from the road and the farms and the factory. They do her fine, she thinks, and take her where she wishes to go, which is all a body can ask of a pair of feet. Anyway, she hates shoes.

She sits in the back row of the church, listening to the half-drunk pastor intoning on the virtues of Virtue, and of the beloved Minister—the Parent of Virtue—in his strange, dark tower in the centre of the country. Everyone loves the Minister. It's the law.

The entire town packs itself into the pews. Church services are required. Of course they are; how else would the population be reminded to pay homage to the Minister, if it weren't for required services, the daily adulations, his face on the money or everywhere else, or the National Radio Broadcasts blasting into each home at four hour intervals without hesitation, inclination or volume control? What better way to be roused in the middle of the night, to interrupt the nightmares of sleep, than to be yanked into consciousness with the sweaty, panicked, screaming name of the Minister in the mouth?

The people of the town sit in the church, straight-backed, shoulder-to-shoulder on a rough-hewn bench. To all appearances, they are attentive. It is a practiced attention.

Pastor Jenkins clears his throat. His jowls are grey, his eyes hooded, and his hands shake. He hurts. He longs for a drink; this is obvious to everyone.

The junk man's daughter gazes at his face and feels her heart breaking in her body with compassion. She feels his need as if it were her own, and experiences the deepness of the pastor's ache in her bones. She traces his face with her gaze, studiously imagining a tumbler full of whiskey—all amber and gold—sliding down his throat, hot and cold all at once. She imagines the heaviness on his tongue, the squeeze of his throat as he swallows. She watches as his tongue darts across his lips. She watches as he swallows. To her satisfaction, she notes the creeping flush of his cheeks and the sudden steadying of his voice. The smell of whiskey wafts through the pews.

She smiles.

No one notices.

The pastor continues with his sermon.

Mr. Brilange and his wife are late as usual. The junk man's daughter has to pull her knees tight to her chest so the Brilanges may pass by her in the pew. She grabs her bare feet and makes herself as small as she can, in case she is bumped.

The Brilanges don't see her now, but they *have* before, a couple of times, and they do not like her. Mr. Brilange called her a guttersnipe, and Mrs. Brilange called her a tramp. Doesn't matter; the junk man's daughter loves them. She loves everyone. She can't help it.

31

According to the rules, the pastor would be required to make note of the tardiness, though that particular statute, like many rules from the Capitol, has a tendency to be routinely ignored. They are remote here, a backwater; often forgotten. They do their best not to make waves, especially recently.

Especially since the onset of the … *well*, no one knows what to call it, and certainly no one mentions it. Little quirks started appearing around town ten years earlier: The roof that won't leak, despite the gaping holes; the jug that makes any water run clean; the old woman who can tell if someone's lying just by touching their right earlobe; the little boy who can talk to horses and sheep and birds. Right useful, that little skill.

No one calls these things magic.

How could it be magic?

Magic is against the law.

Martina Strange, two rows up, starts to cough. The cough tears through her chest and sends rhythmic waves coursing over her back. No one responds. She's been coughing for years, and she is old. It's only a matter of time.

The junk man's daughter stands up. She snakes through the pews. No one notices. She lays her hands on the old woman's back. She is standing so close to the man sitting behind Mrs. Strange, that the girl is practically in the man's lap. He doesn't notice. The junk man's daughter feels a pleasant heat between the skin of her hands and the coat of the woman. She feels the coat thin and give way, and the flannel shirt and the thermal underwear, and the thin jersey that probably belonged to the old woman's husband years ago.

She presses until she is skin to skin. There is, the girl notices, a cancer wedged in the lung—black and twisted and oozing. The heat on her hands is so hot, she can feel her fingertips start to blister. She doesn't move, and instead closes her eyes.

The woman shudders.

She lurches.

She gasps, clasps her hand to her mouth, and coughs so hard it sounds as though it came from the centre of the earth. Once, twice, and at that third cough, out of her mouth flies a bird—black, twisted and angry, with oozing pustules for eyes and talons gripping something bloody.

The congregation gasps. The bird hovers in front of Mrs. Strange—all rage and malevolence—spirals four times inside the four walls of the church, and with a tremendous squawk, shatters the third window on the east side, and flies out of sight.

There is a spangle of glass on the ground.

There are bloody, black feathers on people's laps. Every mouth hangs open.

The junk man's daughter still doesn't move. Her skin pricks and tingles. She bites her lips and presses her hands to her chest—all hope and anticipation. Still no one notices her. The entire congregation holds its breath. They wait. A beat passes. And a beat. And a beat.

Oh, for crying out loud, the girl wants to shout, *say something. Notice your life.*

A beat. A beat.

A bird just flew out of a dying woman's mouth, for God's sake! You have the proof on your damn laps. The world that you have inherited isn't the world that you have to claim. There is so much, so much more. But she says nothing and they say nothing, and eventually pastor Jenkins resumes where he left off. The girl sighs and returns to her seat. What else can she do? Shake them?

Marla the egg woman arrives and sits next to the junk man's daughter, just as the service concludes. The pastor gives the egg woman a deferential nod and clears his throat. Drunk or not, there is no way he would report Marla. He wouldn't dare.

Marla lays her basket on the ground, and gives a sidelong glance to the barefoot girl with the cast-off clothes, and the coat that should be burned by the smell of it. She shakes her head. Reaching over, she lays her hand on the girl's knee and gives it a squeeze.

"Hello, my Sparrow," she whispers. Marla can always see her. For as long as she can remember. The girl doesn't know why this is, but she appreciates it all the same.

The junk man's daughter lays her head on the egg woman's shoulder. There is so much love coursing through her body that she can hardly bear it. She loves the town and each person in it, though few of them love her back. And her love rattles and heats inside of her. It thrums against her skin and wrinkles her bones. It hurts, this love. It exhausts her. She will need to take a break in a moment, find a dark corner filled with quiet and loneliness, and *thinking*.

She has *so much* to think about.

"Where's your papa?" Marla asks.

"Feeling poorly," the girl says with a shrug.

Marla snorts. "You mean drunk," she says.

The junk man's daughter doesn't respond. She gazes at the backs of each head in the pew, lets her eyes graze along their straight spines, their aching shoulders, their swollen joints. She looks inside and sees empty bellies, worried minds, broken hearts. She wants to gather each one in her arms, love them to bits. She wants to help them, heal them, give them strong backs and clear eyes and loud voices. She wants their lives to overflow.

She can do it, too. She knows she can. She just has to figure out how.

The egg woman narrows her eyes.

"Just what are you up to, girl?" she says.

The junk man's daughter closes her eyes. She takes a long, slow breath in through her nose and holds it in for a moment. She turns to the egg woman, who instantly clutches her heart. She loves that girl so much it hurts. Her young face is warm, and flushed and shining.

"Something wonderful," the girl whispers. She kisses the egg woman on the cheek and slips out of the church. No one notices her go.

No one speaks to Mrs. Strange, nor do they comment on the deepening flush of her cheeks, the growing glow of good health and vigour.

No one mentions the bird.

At least, not yet.

10

THEN

THERE WERE ONLY TWENTY MAGIC CHILDREN BORN THAT YEAR.
Nineteen, if you subtract the one that died.

The constable made a show of holding the dead baby's mother
down as the Inquisitor weighed the tiny corpse, took photographs of
the magic mark curling out of the navel, and filled out the forms in
triplicate. But really, it was only a show. The woman in the birthing
bed was drugged and exhausted. Her soul was worn thin. She gave
no sign of resistance, no indication of struggle. Her shoulders
were damp clay in his hands, and her eyes were flat, and dull as
porridge.

"Come now," the constable had said. "That's enough," as though
just by play-acting with the mother he could spark a little life out of
her. If she fought him, he reasoned, maybe she would heal.

"I have authorisation from the Minister," the Inquisitor said, "to
gift to your family the full amount, even though his Excellency will
be deprived the assistance of this once-blessed child." He adjusted
his glasses on his nose. "It is most generous."

"Most," whispered the woman in the birthing bed, "generous."

Even her voice was a cold, dead thing. "Can I have my baby back now?"

The Inquisitor squinched his face as though smelling something foul. "Of course not," he said incredulously. "You have been paid. The procedures are done. The child is marked, therefore the child belongs to the Minister."

"But—" the woman on the bed began.

The Inquisitor interrupted her. "Young lady, it doesn't matter whether or not she is alive. Death, in the case of magic children, is irrelevant. A magic child is a government child, and your government thanks you. It says so on this form."

Within seconds, the mother in the bed sprang to life. Her dull eyes burned and her ashen cheeks flushed.

It was so sudden, so abrupt, that it seemed to the constable to be nothing short of a miracle. *She lives!* The constable nearly sobbed in relief. He was new to the job, and he could tell already that there was a reason why no one else wanted it. Still, better he do it than some Minister's stooge from the Capitol. This was *his* town, after all.

The woman twisted this way and that. Her feet were still in their straps, and she would not be able to undo them without a nurse. "Take these off," she shouted.

"As a spokesperson for our precious Minister and his government—"

She spat. "To hell with the government." She punched the Constable in the eye. "To hell with the goddamned Minister. Give me my dead baby, damn it."

The Inquisitor gaped in horror. "Language, lady," he sputtered. "This is a hospital! Keep your heresy to yourself."

She thrashed and bit. The constable got a fingernail in the eye, teeth marks on his bicep, a knee in his groin. He groaned.

"Constable," the Inquisitor said, "please use the cuffs for the wrists

37

of the heretic traitor, and deal with her at a later time. I expect you know what to do with this kind of law-breaking."

The constable did, of course, though he suspected that it was different than what the Inquisitor had in mind. They had their own ways of dealing with things, out here in the hinterlands. It was better to keep that information as quiet as possible.

Much later, in the constable's office, the box containing the dead baby sat on the desk. It had sat there for hours. The constable opened the lid, and closed it again, wrinkling his eyebrows.

The baby was still dead. That was certain.

The Inquisitor stood next to the wall, a telephone perched between his ear and his shoulder. For some reason, his communicator had ceased functioning normally, and he was forced to humble himself with the substandard technologies of the outlying towns; as if his job wasn't hard enough.

The constable opened the lid of the box again, grunted, and closed it.

"Yes," the Inquisitor said. "Yes, yes, yes." A pause. "Of course I'll hold."

The constable nearly jumped out of his skin. He opened the box. Closed it with a smack. Shook his head.

"Yes," the Inquisitor said, "I understand the Minister is very upset, and for good reason. Imagine that woman. Giving birth to a dead baby, and a magic baby, of all things. It is an insult that cannot be borne. But there is still a question of the corpse itself." Pause. "Yes, I'll hold."

The constable leaped from his chair and started pacing the room. He shot a glance at the box on the desk, and gave a sidelong glance at the Inquisitor on the phone. He slid his gaze back to the box.

"Is there a problem?" the Inquisitor said.

The constable shook his head. "Nope," he said with a grimace. "Nope, I don't believe so."

It took three days for the Inquisitor to get an answer. Three days the dead baby sat in that box. The constable didn't sleep a wink. He normally slept on a cot that he kept in the back corner of his office, but instead of sleeping, he spent the last three days sitting straight up, his back against the wall, his knees bent under his chin. Staring.

And he heard it.

And he heard it again.

He rubbed his eyes, rubbed his mouth, shook his head. "Stop being an idiot," he told himself. Still, he did not sleep. Still, he kept watch.

Finally, the Inquisitor received an answer. Not a particularly *good* answer, but an answer all the same.

"Come now," the Inquisitor said. "You will accompany me so you may co-sign the form."

The two men, along with the phalanx of soldiers, walked to the rubbish heap.

There it is again!

Don't they hear it?

When they reached the entrance to the heap at the edge of town, the Inquisitor gave the constable a hard look. "Well," he said, "go on."

"Go on what?" the constable said.

There! Why doesn't anyone notice?

"Throw the trash on the heap."

"*What?*" the constable sputtered. He clutched the box to his chest. "That's a horrible thing."

"No," the Inquisitor said, "those are our orders. There were nineteen magic children born. They have no names. They do not exist. They live only for the Minister. This one—the twentieth—is a dud. So, the trash heap, then." The Inquisitor was a short man, but he drew himself up, attempted an imperious expression. He pointed to the heap with one, long finger. "Honestly, where do you think the *rest* of them end up? It's not like there's a graveyard for magic children. It would rile people up. Think it through, man."

The constable thought he might be sick.

"But," the Inquisitor added, "not the box. Cardboard is expensive."

"It's been fouled," the constable said, and it had; the tiny body had already started to leak.

"No matter. It's still usable. Go on now."

The constable walked slowly out onto the heap, his heart like a boulder in his chest. He knelt down, and scooped the baby out of the box. It would be unrecognisable soon. The flesh would corrupt and loosen and fall, the sinews would be picked away and the bones would bleach until they shone.

The child never was, and that was that.

But as the constable walked away, holding the reeking box as far away from his body as he could, he heard it once again.

A child's voice. He couldn't tell where it came from—the air, the birds, the drizzling sky, or the trash under his feet—but the sound was unmistakable. The gurgling voice of a little baby.

And it was laughing.

11

NOW

MARLA DOESN'T HEAR FROM THE JUNK MAN OR HIS DAUGHTER for weeks after the bird incident.

No one mentions what happened at church that day. They talk about the weather. They talk about the increased hours at the factory. They talk about grandbabies and funerals, and whether they should plant corn or soybeans this year.

All the while, in the silent spaces between neighbour and neighbour—*the bird, the bird, the bird.* It rings and spins, and ricochets between mouth and mouth, heart and heart, eye and eye, though all in silence. A storm is mentioned—*the bird.* A wedding is announced—*the bird.* A potluck is planned—*the bird, the bird, the bird.* That foul-tempered cancer-bird haunts darkened corners, hidden alleys and littered streets. It is everywhere, and it is silent. No one mentions the bird. Everyone thinks about the bird.

But, bird or no bird, one thing is for sure: Martina Strange is healed. *Healed.* For the first time in her life, she breathes and breathes without hack or hesitation or wheeze. Her cheeks are pink, her eyes bright, and weirdly, her seven missing teeth have suddenly re-erupted in her mouth—straight and white and shining. She walks back and forth between her hovel of a house to her job as a charge-packer at the munitions factory with a gravity of bearing, an integrated sense of deep joy. She walks like a prophet, a sage, a queen.

Marla the egg woman doesn't know what to make of it, and she worries.

Because under her feet she can feel it.

A buzz.

A rumble.

Getting bigger every day.

"My Sparrow, my Sparrow, my Sparrow," she whispers. "What are you planning?"

Except her heart does not say *what are you planning*. Her heart says, *don't leave me*, and it does not say *my Sparrow*. Her heart says, *my child*.

12

THEN

THERE WAS A TIME, SO LONG AGO THAT THE MINISTER COULD hardly remember it, that he was a boy. A *child.* There was a memory that he treasured above all others, of standing with his mother in a field and looking up at the stars.

There, his mother said, *a planet, and there,* she pointed high above, *the largest of all known stars.*

There, she tracked her finger across the sky, *a bit of magic. If you can find where it lands, then none of us will ever die. Not me, not your father, not you. We will live forever.*

In his memory of that moment, his mother's face was young and beautiful, made more so by the long thin scar that began at her left temple and arced prettily down her cheek, hooking over the curve of her jaw and ending at the centre of her windpipe. The Minister, as a boy, loved that scar, and he tracked its trajectory every night with his index finger, just as his mother tracked the falling star.

When he was young enough to assume that his hopes were powerful enough to true themselves upon the face of the world, and old enough to understand loss, both his parents donned their uniforms and marched off with most of the other parents of his acquaintance, and headed into war. He had no idea what *war* was, and assumed it was similar to the wars that he fought with the other children in the neighbourhood, in which the only casualties were the occasional broken arm, and a few tortured pet dogs that were not to be mentioned later.

His mother was so beautiful in her high boots and fatigues. The moment before they left, both his parents gathered him in their arms and kissed him before marching away. The Minister sat on his grandfather's lap and waved and waved, and counted the days until his parents would return and life would become normal once again.

It did not, alas. His mother, thanks to an inopportune step, had been blown to bits. There was nothing to bury. Only his father came back. The Minister never forgave him.

In the ensuing years, the Minister spent most nights in the backyard, looking up at the stars. He couldn't bear to be under the same roof as his father, who couldn't bear to look upon the face of his son. War had become commonplace in those days, and blackouts were a way of life. The roof of the night sky, therefore, was unencumbered by leaking lights or passing cars. While his neighbours crouched and shivered in the darkness, the boy Minister watched the workings of the heavens on full display before him—each glittering body smartly following their courses like soldiers. He kept records and drew maps. He delighted in their punctual grace. Each time an asteroid fell, he traced it with his finger along the curve of the sky, and thought of his mother.

There, her voice in his mind, *a bit of magic.*

The Minister became convinced that his mother's words were true, and he became convinced that perhaps he *should* have found the place where the falling star fell, and perhaps if he *did* that he might have been able to save her.

44

Perhaps there was a way to prevent *himself* from ever dying, he mused. It was a thing worth wishing for, after all. Freedom from death, from erasure, from oblivion, and once he thought it, he began to want it, and then it was all he wanted. Well, almost all. He held his finger in the darkness before him, and traced the curve of his mother's scar. He would never forget it. It haunted his dreams.

Maybe I can bring her back.

13

NOW

THEY ARE TWO TOWNS OVER, THE SPARROW AND HER FATHER, and they are wet through, and chilled to the bone.

"How can there be no whiskey?" the junk man moans. "There is always whiskey."

It's true. There is always whiskey. Or at least there has been whiskey in abundance for the last fifteen years. There have been many things in abundance for the last fifteen years.

The junk man has theories about this. He has memories about a miraculous baby, but they are faded and fuzzy, as wobbly and patched-together as his own dear cart. He puts his arm around his daughter, who wraps her arms around his middle. She is the only thing that's real.

The rain pours harder. The Sparrow pulls her father close, helping him scoot further into the lee of the wagon, their backs curving under the edge. Surely it will stop soon. Four identical chickens—all Most Remarkable Hens, and all named Midge—peck at the ground under the cart. From time to time, they touch the tops of their heads to the girl's back, as though reminding themselves that she is still there.

They love her. *So much.*

The face of the Minister gazes over the town. A massive billboard. They are everywhere. His smile is practiced, his skin is slick as resin. Even from here, the Sparrow can smell the formaldehyde and camphor on his breath.

The billboards will be useful. The junk man's daughter has a plan, *but not yet,* her heart pleads. *I'm not ready.* She leans her cheek on the bony angles of her father's shoulders and tries to breathe him in. She cannot leave him yet.

People rush by with their homemade umbrellas or their oilcloths, or their remnants of old plastic sheets. They see the junk man, but they do not greet him. They do not offer shelter. They have heard the stories. They have considered writing reports, but they fear incriminating themselves. After all, the junk man has been selling his wares in their jurisdiction for years. *Years.*

A troop of soldiers—twelve in all—marches by, the mud splattering in the wake of their boots. Their faces are covered. The faces of the soldiers are always covered. On the day of their initiation, their bright Interfaces are fused to their cheekbones and linked to their eyes—allowing everything they hear, smell, see, and think to be instantly uploaded and searchable by the Minister himself. Each Interface has a scar, starting at the temple, arcing prettily across the cheek and hooking under the limit of the jaw.

The Interfaces look ever so much like the Minister's mother. No one knows this. No one except for the Sparrow. It only makes her love him the more.

"I just don't understand it," the junk man says, shivering again. "How can it be *gone?*"

"It's a mystery, Papa," the Sparrow says, but it's not. In truth, she dumped it out. It's an experiment—one that, currently, is going poorly. "You'll adjust to its absence in a bit, I'm sure."

It had been 32 hours exactly since his last drink. He is not adjusting

47

well. He is yellow and grey and woozy; a shadow of himself. He shakes and groans, sweats and shivers. He cannot hold water. His heart strains in his chest.

"Just hold on." *You need to be okay if I am not here,* her heart pleads with him.

Not if, says a voice deep in her soul, *when.*

"I am so hot, my child, and yet I am cold. I am dying, or perhaps I am dead."

"If so," she squeezes harder, "perhaps it is temporary." She smiles at him. She is not a particularly pretty girl, but he loves her face—its over-wide forehead and over-small nose. He loves each freckle and those black, beady, glittering eyes.

"Temporarily dead," he muses. "I remember…" He holds his breath. He presses his hand to his chest.

The junk man's daughter feels an opening in her heart. It is made of light. It is not death she fears—indeed, why should she?—but it is the thought of her own oblivion that keeps her up at night. There are so few people who see her, who notice her, and most that do forget her within a moment.

To be remembered by somebody.

To be longed for.

To be missed.

This is her only hope. It is the only thing she wants.

"Come on, Papa," she whispers. "Temporarily dead. There is more to the story. It's in there somewhere. You can do it."

In a flash, the junk man remembers. He remembers everything.

14

THEN

THE CONSTABLE ASKED MARLA THE EGG WOMAN TO SEE TO THE mother of the dead baby.

"I won't do it," Marla said.

"She won't see me, that's for damn sure," the constable said. "And someone needs to look after her. After all, considering your history—"

Marla slapped him as hard as she could across his right cheek, and then she slugged him in his belly. The constable wrapped his arms around his middle and doubled over.

No wonder no one wanted this stupid job, he thought.

Marla sighed. "Fine," she said. "I'll do it. Never mention my history again."

She walked away.

People didn't mention Marla's history. It was too sad.

The mother had taken no food or drink, save liquor, for over a week. When Marla arrived, the woman was in bed. The room reeked of sweat, sick and an overripe chamber pot. Her husband gave up days ago, opting to drown his grief in the company of men at the tavern, rather than in the presence of his raving wife.

Marla took the pitcher to the pump and filled it. She emptied the chamber pot and changed the sheets, and opened the windows to let in the day. The mother of the dead child scowled and howled and made a feeble attempt at fighting, but she was simply too weak.

Anyway, no one could best Marla in a fight. No woman, no man, no soldier. No one.

Finally, when the grieving mother was in a clean gown on clean sheets, Marla propped her up on a pillow and started spoon-feeding a soup with eggs, chicken and chervil; easy to digest, good for the soul.

The mother sipped it dutifully.

Finally: "You had one, didn't you?" the mother said. "A magic child."

Marla took a long breath through her nose. Her face was stone. She didn't answer.

"How old were you?" the mother said.

Marla closed her eyes. "Fifteen," she said. "I was fifteen."

The woman's eyes were red and damp. "Hell of a thing," she said, and Marla nodded. "Yours still alive?"

Marla stood. She needed to get out. Right now. She forced herself to stay. Turning to the woman in the bed, she held her eyes for a long time.

"There's no way to know. They don't exist, remember?" But the woman's face was pleading, and insistent. Marla sighed. "Probably not."

She filled up the water jug one more time, hid the whiskey and made sure there were enough foodstuffs nearby. She kissed the mother on each cheek and told her that every day would be a little easier.

A lie, of course.

She left without another word.

She did not tell her that her breasts still leaked for a child who went away forever.

She did not tell her that her heart, once big, passionate and full of heat, was now a tight, tiny stone, rattling in her cold, empty chest.

She did not tell her that every night in her dreams she saw her girl, her taken girl—pale lips, milky eyes—at the top of a dark tower, flung out against the spangle of stars in a limitless sky.

She did not tell her that every night she dreamed of flowers. Red flowers, red flowers, red, red, red, red.

15

NOW

THE JUNK MAN'S DAUGHTER SLIDES ALONG THE BACK OF THE LOW, one-roomed building that houses the Constable's office.

The alley lights are out again—energy crisis. It is always an energy crisis. She appreciates the dark. Pressing her hands against the wall, she curls her fingers into the bricks. The sun is down and the moon isn't up yet. The night air is a puckering cold, but the wall is still warm, and so are her hands. She can hear the Constable inside, explaining things to the Inquisitor.

"I don't care what you think you've heard, sonny," she hears the old man say, "there ain't been a whiff of magic anywhere in the county, nigh on fifteen years. Not a drop. Now you can write that down on your report and send it on up to your superiors. You got bad information is all, and not the first time, neither."

A scribble of pen on paper.

An old man's harrumph.

The junk man's daughter leans her cheek against the radiant bricks and inhales the scent of sun, clay and smoke. Dust from the stockyards; the oily belch of the munitions factory down the road. The brick keeps a record of the town's life in smells. She smiles. She loves her home. She loves it *so much*. Despite everything. She bounces a couple of times to steady herself, and then she begins to climb.

The Minister's many faces loom on the top of every building— paper eyes, paper lips. They are large, faded, and garishly lit, as though watching the town. The Minister is always watching, with his smooth face and his white teeth and his rigid smile. There are only eighteen buildings in town, and thus there are also eighteen Ministers of varying sizes, the largest of which sits atop the Constable's office.

It is terribly large.

In this, the largest of the Minister's faces, the dear leader does not smile. He does not show his teeth. His eyes are wide. His lips curl in. He is frightened, she thinks, or angry. He is a child lost in the wood, a supplicant at the feet of a cruel and unfeeling god. The rims of his eyes are wet. His prominent cheekbones have a greenish pallor. She closes her eyes as she climbs and feels her heart skip a beat.

The junk man's daughter loves this billboard best, and she loves the Minister, though he does not know it. She shimmies up the brace-work behind the Minister's face, as clever as a spider, and hooks around to the catwalk along the bottom rim.

"There were only two babies in the county born with the mark last time round, and one of them died before it took its first breath. You know it. You saw 'em. You held that dead baby in your own two hands and you made me throw it in the trash heap to be burned." The Constable smashes his fist on the desk. The mugs and paperclips rattle and fall. His voice is loud. Full of rage.

The Inquisitor says nothing. He only scribbles.

"You think I don't remember? I was there, dammit. You took the pictures, ran the tests and filled out your goddamned forms, and that was that." Each word is an accusation. "And now you're wasting my time on rumours? Please, all this hubbub's a lot of old tosh, and you know it."

She can hear the worry in the Constable's voice, hiding under the righteous anger and indignation, and she knows it is for her. The Constable's one for secrets, that's for sure, and he's one of a precious few what gives a rat's nethers over whether she lives or dies. Which is why she feels—in all truth and sincerity—a great sorrow for what she is about to do. She has never wanted anyone to get in trouble.

She closes her eyes and takes a deep breath.

"You can interview the whole damn town if you want to," says the Constable's voice. It is heightened now, and loud. He is a man to be reckoned with, even when he is lying. "But it's the same. You won't find nothin' when there's nothin' to find. Unlicensed magician, my *eye*."

The junk man's daughter feels it first in her anklebones. A buzz and heat. She removes four strands of hair from her head and, with loops and skilful knots, ties them into the shape of a butterfly. The buzzing sensation crawls its way through her bones. It is in her knees, then her hips. It inches up her spine. The butterfly made of hair is motionless in her hand. The buzz reaches her shoulders and down her arms, and spreads upward into her skull. It is in her fingers, her jaw, her teeth. She blinks bright floaters out of her eyes. Her eyelashes begin to singe.

She places the butterfly made of hair on her tongue and gently presses her lips together. She puffs out her cheeks and closes her eyes, and feels that unpleasant buzz heat its way through her muscles and organs. She feels it crawling across her skin like the scuttle of a thousand ants. She is covered. She is burning. She is so alive.

She opens her mouth wide and sticks out her tongue, and it begins.

The butterflies shoot out in threes. They are large, luridly coloured, and glowing. They have bright eyes, hot antennae, wings that could heat a kitchen on a winter morning.

Fifteen butterflies. Eighteen. Twenty-one.

Her body shudders and shakes. Her eyes water and weep.

Thirty-six. Thirty-nine. Forty-two.

Her skin burns, her teeth burn, her tongue may never be the same.

One hundred and two. One hundred and five.

The butterflies hover over her head in a bright cloud. They shake the air. By the time the three-hundredth butterfly (the largest of them all, with electric-blue wings) emerges from her choking throat, she slumps onto the slats, utterly spent.

The butterflies await their orders.

"The eyes," she gasps, her voice barely a whisper. "Infect the eyes."

The butterflies need no other encouragement. They fly, fast as missiles into the open eyes of each Minister, disappearing into the depths of ink and paper.

"Well," she hears the Inquisitor say, "thank you for your time."

"Make sure you stop at the baker's before you go," the constable's voice says. "Bring a pie home for the missus. You won't regret it."

The eyes of each Minister burn black as coal. They glow red, then gold, then purple. They pulse and swell.

"I'll be sure to make a note of your cooperation in my report."

"I'd appreciate that. We all serve at the Minister's pleasure."

The largest butterfly stays with the girl. It rests on her chest, wrapping its wings over her body like a blanket. She shivers and heaves. Above her, the eyes of the Ministers brighten and beam. She can feel the vibration worming through the air.

Though she is terribly weak, she smiles. She lets her left hand drift over the luminous body of the butterfly, stroking it tenderly. *It's working*, she thinks. *I knew it.*

The Inquisitor wears his visor and keeps his eyes on the papers secured in his clipboard. He fusses over forms signed in triplicate, in figures and diagrams and the proper terminology. He knows that careers are made, stagnated and destroyed on words, and that a single misplaced comma can hang a man. Indeed, it happens all the time. He remembers his less careful colleagues with a shudder. He is fastidious for a reason. He has held this job now for eighteen years; almost a record. The Inquisitor jabs his last period with a flourish and does not look up.

Instead, he exits the building, slides into the back seat of the long, black car waiting for him outside the Constable's office, and raps on the glass separating the driver from the back of the car. The driver clicks it in gear and allows its girth to glide silently down the quiet street.

The Inquisitor does not stop for pie.

The Constable crosses his arms and watches the silent car disappear into the dark. He draws in a long slow breath of cold night air and looks up at the glowing eyes of the Ministers. He sees a growing brightness, and then a burst of energy shooting across the quiet street from eye to eye to eye, making a multi-pointed web over his head.

He sighs deeply, rubbing his arthritic hand over the loosening folds of his face. He needs a shave. He always needs a shave. He looks back up at the slumped figure of the girl on the catwalk, her butterfly still wrapped protectively around her chest. He shakes his head and goes inside to place a phone call.

The telephone on the wall is an ancient thing—heavy black plastic, a twirling wire that attracts dust. He dials the number he knows by heart and braces himself.

"Yep," he says, "got a little sparrow on the roof." He waits. "There's been a development." He holds his breath and nods. "She did indeed." He listens to the other line, and holds the receiver away from his ear for a bit, wincing. "Well, there's no call for that kind of language," he says. "Channel was already open, and we both knew it. Been open for a long time. She just opened it more. Well, a lot more. Fool girl. Don't matter either way. Secret's out. Someone blabbed. Don't know who, but someone did, no mistake, and now we've got a whole mess of trouble coming our way." He waits a bit more, and rests his forehead against the wall. He's getting too old for this sort of thing. "Yep, I'll get her down. Why don't you come and collect her when you can? Bring the other fool, too, assuming he's sober enough to stand."

Outside, the light emanating from the eyes of the Ministers is so bright that he can't see the stars. It's a pity; a little starlight might clear his head or soothe his soul. It usually did. He shrugs, rears back, and with more agility than would seem possible for a man of his age, leaps halfway up the building and clings like an insect to the bricks. He scuttles the rest of the way, scoops up the girl and her butterfly in one arm, and rappels back down, leap after downward leap, gripping the bricks with both feet and one hand. He lands on the ground, as light and soundless as dust.

He brings her inside, locking the door behind him, and lays her gently on the cot in his office, crossing the room to put the kettle on.

"Huh," he says. The constable stares at his hands, utterly amazed. He curls his fingers into tight fists and stretches them out as far as they will go. His arthritis is utterly gone. His joints are unswollen and loose for the first time in twenty years, and his performance on the side of the building is a thing he never has been able to do—even when he was young and strong.

What's more, he hadn't even *thought* about it. His body knew what it could do before he did. He removes his eyeglasses and scans the room, blinking all the while. Crisp, sharp lines; details standing stark in relief. He slides the spectacles into a drawer, closing it with a decisive click, wondering if he would ever need them again.

"Good god, girl," he whispers to the sleeping child on the cot. "What did you go and do?"

16

· THEN

ON THE MORNING AFTER THE BORO COMET FINALLY VANISHED from the night sky, not to return for another quarter-century, the junk man—the man with a wobbly cart and the hand-patched boots who smelled always of grave mould and vomit, whiskey and piss, the man who came through town every Saturday from the West Road and left every Monday by the East—found the dead child lying on the rubbish heap; the child with the magic mark.

He wasn't looking for a child—living or dead—nor did he trouble himself with the national frenzy over the Boro Comet, whose arrival always meant trouble. He had better things to do, frankly.

The junk man began searching the rubbish heap, picking up treasures as he went: a possibly-gold chain; a perfectly-good shoe; a solicitor's briefcase, likely taken before the gentleman in question was thrown into the river with stones tied to his ankles. It was a dangerous profession these days, soliciting.

There were fliers, too. Signs, banners, all regarding that troublesome Boro Comet with its foolishness and woe. He kicked a banner with his hand-patched boot.

The junk man wanted nothing to do with the drama, and was, instead, picking his way through the debris on the rubbish heap to find something forgotten and cast-off, and *valuable*; a bit of treasure in the muck.

The soldiers had left already, carrying the other baby—the living baby—with all the pomp and ceremony necessary for a child who mattered so very much to the beloved Minister, in a silk-lined basket, leaving a sack of money, government bonds and gold commemorative coins (along with violent insinuations and vague threats) with both grieving families. There were only twenty born that year in the whole country—nineteen if you subtract the one that died. That's the lowest number in memory. No more babies for the Minister. Not for another twenty-five years.

The junk man sang as he picked through the heap. His feet quivered with a bit of a suppressed jig and his fingers began to itch. He loved the rubbish heap. You never know what a man might find in there. It's how he found a ring so valuable that it kept him in butter and beef for over a year, and the deed to the land where his shack now stands. Tools, outlawed books, loose change, mostly-operational eyeglasses, a set of false teeth.

And then a baby. A baby that had been—not five minutes before— as dead as can be. He had *seen* it. The thing was a days-old corpse, its eyes pecked out by ravens, its body grey, foul and leaking.

Then, without warning, the child curled its lips. It stuck out its putrefied tongue and crinkled its cheeks. It began to whimper, then cry. It blinked and blinked, raking its eyelids across the fleshy sockets again and again, until two bright eyes suddenly appeared, as shiny as new pennies. Its cheeks plumped and pinked, the skin suddenly glowing with good health and vitality. It breathed, blew bubbles. A rosebud mouth sought a nipple, and four tiny limbs kicked and flailed with hunger, cold and rage.

It was warm, ruddy, and *alive*.

Impossible.

The junk man fell to his knees, clutched his heart. His first thought was to dash the child's head against the rock—surely it was possessed, or it was a demon, or an apparition dreamed up by some wronged customer to cause him to lose his mind before losing his life. Clearly, it would devour his flesh, suck his brain, and go carousing through the countryside finding innocents to maul. He approached the child cautiously. He rubbed his mouth with the back of his hand and sank into a crouch, resting his bottom on the heels of his boots. He settled his face into a suspicious stare. The baby, hardly noticing him, began to wail.

It sounded like a baby.

It smelled like a baby.

The child was naked. A girl. She hiccupped in her loneliness and grief. The magic mark curled like a snail's shell out from her navel. It gave off a bit of a pale glow. She brought her fist to her mouth and sucked it desperately.

Oh, she was terribly alone. He cupped his hand over the top of her fragile skull, and felt the gentle beating of her fontanelle pulse, like the wing of a bird.

The junk man felt something stir within him. The heart that he did not know that he possessed eased into an unused groove and clicked neatly and surely into place, like a coin into a slot. His eyes sprang wide. He shuddered and gasped. He was alive in a way he never knew before. He pressed his index finger to her palm, and felt the pincher grip of those tiny fingers. The tendrils growing around his heart, holding it in place, pulled in tight, and everything was clear.

He cleared his throat and looked levelly at the child. He had never spoken to a baby before, and was unsure how to begin.

"Good god, girl," he said, "it's not every day that you meet a body what can outwit a pack of soldiers. Good on you." He shook the child's hand solemnly, and looked behind him to see if he was being observed.

There was no one on the rubbish heap—save for a mostly-drunk junk man and a recently-dead baby. He found an old bed sheet, and tore it into strips, binding the baby to his body. The child calmed. She abandoned her fist, opting to suck on his filthy shirt for nourishment instead. Buttoning his coat over the baby, the junk man took a deep breath and pushed his cart down the road.

The child squawked twice. He began to walk with a bit of a sway, rocking her with the swish of his body. "Hush now, little sparrow," he said. "I'll get you fed soon enough. That or you'll feed the buzzards again. We'll see."

He headed to the far side of town and down the path into a thicket of wood, toward the egg woman's house. She would know what to do. She usually did.

17

NOW

Marla the egg woman arrives at the Constable's office just before midnight. The junk man follows closely behind, pushing his wobbly cart, emptied of its usual cargo.

He grumbles. She pays him no mind. He grumbles louder.

"Had it all arranged just so," he says. "Just how I liked it."

"Stuff it, old man," the egg woman says without turning around. "This is all your fault." She looks up and sighs. She is being unfair, and she knows it; someone else is at fault.

She glances up and gives the lurid billboards atop each building a hard look. The bright web linking the eyes of the Ministers is starting to fade a bit, but she can feel it all the same; an electric hum in the air, pricks in the skin, something bubbling underground. Like as not, everyone in town can feel it, too. It's only a matter of time before things start happening.

Not that they hadn't been happening already.

The constable's office is dark; she knocks anyway. The old man's face appears in the window, lit by a candle. He grunts, fusses with the chain, and ushers them inside.

"Marla," he says to the egg woman, with a respectful bow. "Sonny," he says to the junk man with his usual derision. The constable calls all men younger than himself 'sonny', but he reserves a special bit of extra scorn for the junk man, *on principle.*

"Who brought the bug?" the junk man slurs, squinching his face at the luminescent butterfly still resting on the girl's chest, as he sways back and forth like a boat in a ceaseless gale. He shakes to clear the drink. It doesn't work. He feels lightheaded and buoyant, as though his feet are only barely touching the earth.

(Which, incidentally, they aren't.)

"Please don't speak unless you can find a way to make yourself less of an idiot, Simon," Marla says. She is the only one in town who calls the junk man by his name. She turns to the constable. "Has it started?" She doesn't know why she asks this; it has clearly started.

"She's done this to me before," the constable says. "Sudden bursts of strength. Wholeness. But never like this, and never for this long. I picked that girl up like she was a bag of feathers, and went up and down the side of the building with my bare hands. Didn't even occur to me to find a ladder, and now, I been leaning down and tying and retying my own shoes. Opening jars without pain. Pushups, hand stands, flying leaps. The whole bit. I even lifted my desk over my head without strain, and that thing is heavier than a truck."

"I see," Marla says, closing her eyes.

The junk man walks (*no; he floats*) to the sleeping girl. He tries to wipe the drunkenness away from his face. The whiskey stink pours from his pores in a cloud, and, suddenly, he feels ashamed. He lays his hand on her forehead, sliding his fingers onto her cheek as though she was still a little child. In his heart, she is always a little child. She feels hot and dry.

"She's sick," he says.

"It'll pass," the egg woman says firmly.

"You don't know that," the constable says, "and you don't know what'll happen next. Us three've been protecting her all these years, and now…" He raises his eyes to the ceiling. "The thought of government soldiers marching into my town is a thing that has kept me up at night ever since the two of you pulled me into this business. In any case, this is where they'll come first, so this is where she needs *not* to be. Get her back to the farm, and maybe get her out of town."

The junk man curls his arms around the sleeping girl. Her body feels lighter than it should, as though she had been filled up with helium. He pulls her to his chest and cradles her like he did when she was a baby.

"Little Sparrow," he croons. "My precious little bird." Though he is unsteady, he doesn't drop her. Marla gives him a look—hard and exasperated and forgiving all at once. She follows him out the door.

Outside, as they lay the girl and her butterfly in the cart, Marla reaches into her basket and hands three eggs to the constable. He tries to decline.

"I couldn't possibly. *Three?* Not during a food shortage."

"You'll eat them and you'll be grateful for it. One's for strength and one's for luck." She nods and turns down the road. The constable stares at his three eggs.

"What's the third one for?" he calls after her.

"Lunacy," the egg woman says without turning around. "It might be our only hope."

18

THEN

At first, the junk man didn't notice anything strange about the recently-dead baby; besides, of course, its de-corpsification.

That, he allowed, was *odd,* and was a thing best not thought about.

In any case, he was the last person to get judgmental or *holier than thou.* Live and let live, that was his philosophy, his heart giving a little thrill at the word *live.*

Live, live, live. He nearly sang it.

Besides, despite the fact that he had seen it with his own eyes, he had difficulty accepting the whole business as fact. *Not really.* She was too alive, too...*wonderful.* It was as though she was only dead *in theory.* A clever trick by a clever girl.

Without meaning to, he leaned in and kissed the wobbly, delicate top of her tiny head. She smelled so good it made him weak inside, and yet *strong,* too; as though he had the strength to do bare-handed battle with legions of soldiers-of-fortune just to protect her. He wanted to do harm to any who might try to harm her. He wanted to find the individuals responsible for throwing a baby—*a baby, for God's sake*—onto a rubbish heap. As though she were, well, *rubbish*.

The very idea.

It enraged him just thinking about it. He wanted to tear out their hearts, rip off their heads and spit upon their graves. He wanted their reputations slandered, their good deeds questioned and their names forgotten by history. He wanted *their* corpses thrown on rubbish heaps. Let them see how they liked it. Actually, no, he enjoyed rubbish heaps as a general rule. Best not pollute them.

The child whimpered. She was *so* hungry.

"Soon, my sweet," the junk man said. "Soon, my little sparrow. You will eat and eat until your blood runs sweet. Sweet in the mouth, sweet in the eyes, sweet in your tiny heart."

Where was this coming from, he wondered. Poetry? Crooning? Great heavens. He had never been a sentimental man. What other strange magicks did this child possess?

He wasn't sure what infants ate when there wasn't a mother to do the job. He had no breasts, of course, so any feeding in the usual way was right out. Milk seemed a reasonable option, but milk from a cow or milk from a goat? Or perhaps a sheep? He had no idea, but the child was hungry, and she must be fed. He worried about her crying—what if someone alerted the authorities? What if someone handed her off to the same soldiers who threw her away? His fear was hot and cold at once. He curled his arm around his precious bundle and walked faster.

He didn't know what family she originally belonged to—most of the pregnant women had been rounded up and stored in an asylum until their due dates came. He could ask around, but not many people in town wanted to talk to the junk man, or anyone, really. You never did know who might be a spy for the government.

He skirted the main road and went along the back byways. He

shot furtive glances at people who did not glance back. If they heard the child crying, they did not show it.

In her little carrier under his shirt, she squawked and kicked and sucked, just like a normal baby. So he sang as he walked, bowing his arms out slightly as he pushed his cart down the ragged road through town.

Out of town, and into that little diagonal trail into the woods that few people knew about. Marla the egg woman liked her privacy and didn't advertise her address. But he and Marla had a history, didn't they? Surely she would be willing to offer advice at the very least?

The egg woman was just exiting the coop when he arrived. She was covered in dust and feathers. She was a wide, well-built woman—low to the ground and stable as a boulder; as reliable as earth.

She set her basket of eggs gently on the ground and glared at the junk man. She curled her meaty hands into fists and took a long, slow breath in through her nose. He was worried this might happen.

"Marla," he said, "you are a sight for sore eyes." He meant it, too. He loved her, once, after all, and once he had a chance to make her happy, and to be made happy in return. But he loved the drink more. And she hated drunks. So it goes.

"What do you want?" she said, as she brushed the chicken debris from her overalls and hair.

"Found something on the rubbish heap today," he said. He was breathless. He was worried. He wanted to show her the child, to have her inspect, evaluate and *love* her, and yet, *not*, at the same time. What if she wanted to take the child from him? What then? He felt a sob bloom in the depths of his throat.

"I'm not interested." She arched her back to crack the kinks out of her spine and tilted her head to the sky, as if just talking to the junk man required divine intervention. She picked up her basket and walked toward the front porch.

"Marla—" he began. The baby's whimper increased to a full wail. The egg woman didn't seem to notice.

"That's enough with the familiarity, thanks. You know the rules." It had been like this for years. Her voice was a brick wall with him, and he was a broken bottle. This is why they never spoke.

"The soldiers," he insisted. "The ones what took the baby with the mark."

"Don't talk about that," she said. "It's too sad."

The junk man knew that she once had a child with the magic mark. She was fifteen—only a child herself. She mentioned it only once, very long ago, and never since.

The baby squawked again. Marla didn't seem to notice.

"Please, um, Madame Egg Gatherer. I really and truly need your help. The baby—" The baby raised her voice to a wail. Still Marla did not notice.

"I will be setting the dogs out soon," she said. "You would be wise to be gone." She disappeared into the house.

The junk man stood on the porch, his head muddled by confusion and drink, and further addled by the loudening wails of the hunger-panicked baby.

He sighed, ran his hand over his face and shook his head to dislodge the clouds in his brain. He unbuttoned his coat and laid it on the ground. Untying the baby's wrappings, he realised one reason for her growing discomfort.

"Poor little thing," he said, "sitting around in your own poo. Unfortunately I know the feeling." He wiped her off with the torn up sheet and laid her on the coat. She spread out her hands, waved her fists, and kicked vigorously with untapped rage.

"Marla," he called.

"Don't call me that, Simon. I have been very clear."

"What kind of milk do you give to a baby?"

"Why on earth do you want to know that?"

"Whatever the best kind is, I'd like to buy it. You sell it, don't you?"

"The dogs are coming out right now, Simon. I would be terribly sad if they ripped your face off, despite everything. But I will comfort myself in knowing that you brought it on yourself." She opened the door and three large dogs came tumbling onto the porch, snarling and snapping.

The junk man rubbed his thumbs on the soles of the baby's feet and moved her legs back and forth. She calmed a bit, hiccupped, and launched a spray of urine straight down onto his bended knee. She smiled.

"Atta girl," the junk man said, utterly delighted.

The dogs stopped their snarling and tilted their heads. The largest of the three leaned down and sniffed the head of the baby. It wagged its tail and whined a bit.

"What on earth?" the egg woman said.

"I told you. It's a baby. Your dogs know better than to attack an infant, thank God. I think I'll keep her around."

Marla slid out the screen door and skirted the sniffing dogs. She glared at the junk man hunched over the coat. "There is nothing on that coat, Simon," she said.

"Close your eyes," he whispered. "Close your eyes and *smell.*"

Knees cracking, the egg woman folded her legs, sitting primly on her heels. She rested her elbows on her thighs and closed her eyes, breathing deeply through her nose.

"Oh," she whispered.

"You see?" he said.

"But..." she opened her eyes. "*Oh!*" A gasp, a shudder, a sigh. And she *saw.* He could tell. Hesitating slightly, she extended her right hand to the magic mark curling from the child's navel. She let her fingers linger there for a moment, each breath shuddering in and out, in and out. She pulled away, pressed her hands to her mouth, and tears leaked into the crinkles around her eyes. *"The poor little thing."*

The junk man gathered the child into the crook of his arm and looked imploringly at the egg woman. "Will you help us?"

The magic mark glittered and glowed. The child sucked madly on her fist.

"Please." He placed his hand on Marla's strong shoulder. He hung on for dear life. She didn't bat his hand away.

She felt her heart start to swell.

19

NOW

After three days of profound, dreamless sleep, the Sparrow emerges from her nest. Her hair is matted and her mouth is raw. There are burn marks on her throat and tongue, and deep cracks in her lips.

She remembers the buzz.

She remembers the butterflies.

She remembers a burning web, an open door and the shiver in her bones, telling her that she wasn't alone anymore. Well, *this should be interesting.*

They are, she realises, at the egg woman's house. She is in the loft—she knows it well. It is a comfortable place—thick quilts, a hand-woven rug, wood walls and a view through the roof-peak window that is shaped like an eye. She knows that Marla is not her mother. Her real mother is the woman with the hollow eyes, the early-grey hair, the face marked by munitions grease, too much drinking and not enough sleep, and too much sorrow for anyone to bear, but Marla has served as her mother-enough for as long as she could remember, and will continue to do so for now.

Many things will do for now.

But not for long.

Her butterfly clings to the far wall, its luminescent wings folded against one another, showing their dusty undersides. It looks like a large, muted flower. It is, she suspects, the only one that survived, and she does not know how long it will live, or whether it grieves its brethren, or whether it will stay with her at all.

She only knows what she *hopes*.

She sits up. She is, she realises, naked under her sheets, and bathed. There is a bowl of water with lemons and mint floating on its surface, and a dish with a small clean sponge resting in its centre. She runs her tongue over the injured inside of her mouth. It tastes slightly of lemons.

How long have I been sleeping? she wonders. She knows that she had been dead once, though she does not remember it. Did she die again? Is her borrowed time nearly gone? She suspects it may be, which is why she feels she must help people while she still breaths; as many as she can.

Which is to say, *everyone*.

There is a flowered dress draped on the chair, and a brush, a pitcher of water and a washbowl on the dresser. There is a pair of soft shoes as well, but those she does not put on. She has never been one for shoes, despite Marla the egg woman's best efforts. She slides over to the ladder and pads downstairs, her butterfly fluttering behind her.

Marla is nowhere to be found. The junk man sprawls his skinny limbs across the couch, his mouth wide open and snoring. The egg woman's dogs have opted to remain in the house, and are sitting at attention, watching the junk man intently. Their ears prick up and their eyes narrow to slits, as though he is a dangerous creature who might need to be subdued at any moment, or torn to shreds.

"Papa," the girl says, her voice a ragged husk of itself.

The dogs whine and thump their tails on the ground. They love the girl—always have. They are old dogs now, impossibly old, but still strong, bright-eyed and spry. It isn't magic, of course it isn't; magic is illegal. Still, whenever she is near them, she can feel her navel glow and heat, and she knows that when the time comes for her to leave town, the dogs will not likely live to see her return. She has accepted this.

In a unified motion, all three dogs slide to their feet and stalk next to the girl, lowering their heads toward the junk man and showing their teeth. He wakes with a start. He stares blearily at the girl, and blinks.

He does not smell of whiskey. He smells instead of pickles, mustard plaster and rosemary tea. Marla has laid down the law, again. The Sparrow finds herself wondering how long it will last.

The junk man coughs. "You're not dead." There is a sob hiding in his voice.

The Sparrow has one too. She knows the ferocity of his love for her, and she shares it. "No, Papa," she says. "I am not dead. Not yet. Where's Marla?"

"Town." He sits, rests his spindly elbows on his bony knees. His fingers are long and delicate as willow twigs, though his knuckles are red and raw from the careless gnaw of his teeth; what is left of his teeth.

"I'm going to follow her. I need to tell her something."

"She told me to tell you to stay put. She made me *promise*." His eyes are red, too; bloodshot and red, and it is not from the withdrawal from the drink. He has been weeping. He will weep again. The girl knows this for sure.

"She will forgive you. Anyway, there is something I need to do."

"My bird, my bird, what do you think you're doing?"

She smiles. He cannot bear it. He presses his hands to his heart.

74

She is, to him, the most beautiful thing in the world. His greatest treasure.

She crinkles her eyes to keep her tears at bay. "The right thing, Papa. I only ever try to do the right thing."

She kisses the top of his head and slips out of the room without another word. Her butterfly clings to her back, its wings appearing as though they are her own, which, the junk man reasons, they kind of *are*.

The dogs follow at her heels.

20

THEN

DESPITE THE EGG WOMAN'S PROTESTATIONS, THE JUNK MAN insisted on bringing the girl wherever he went.

Their Nation was formed in the shape of a dandelion clock—each Province made up of several small towns connected on one circular road, largely left to their own devices—most of the time—and connected to the Capitol by the Main Road, which was heavily guarded and maintained. There was no communication between Provinces, and there was no travel to the Capitol except by express permission of the Minister. There were rumours that it wasn't always so, but no one could say for sure. No one had actually read a history book, after all.

History was another banned subject.

Within the towns of their Province, the junk man enjoyed total freedom of movement. He reported to no one, served no one, needed no one, and slept each night under the stars. With the addition of the baby into his life, only the last bit remained true.

"What if it rains?" Marla protested.

"Then it will rain, and we will be clean," the junk man said, dangling the babe on his knee. He made a carrier that could attach to his back, his front or his hip, depending on what made the child happy. He also built a swing to hover over the cart and a shade to keep her from the cruelties of the sun.

"What if the soldiers come?"

"Let them come," he said, with more conviction than he actually felt. "They can't see her anyway." This had largely been true. While the dogs were aware of the child from the moment they encountered her, no one else seemed to notice that she was there. Both the junk man and the egg woman had tested this, taking the child to the market, to the well, to the monthly Census, and to the required church services, and the results were the same: no one noticed the baby, not even when she cried. She was invisible, inaudible, a cipher.

All's the better, the junk man thought.

But Marla worried. *For what purpose?* her heart fussed. *And for how long?*

At her insistence, the junk man agreed to have the girl stay with the egg woman for one week per month.

"Because someone has to teach her how to keep herself clean and whole," Marla explained. "Someone will have to teach her to read and write and reason. How to mend a sock, make a jacket, keep the wind out and make stew. Someone will have to show her how to take care of her lady bits when they change, and how to shoo the boys away when they come sniffing around. Someone will have to teach her how to protect herself."

The idea that there might, some day, be any lady bits to manage or any wooing boys crossing his path was more than the junk man could bear, and he agreed to the situation. Besides, he reasoned, while he could get reasonably drunk with a baby in tow, he couldn't get *good and drunk,* and the thought of saying farewell to his periodic blackouts was a devastating one. Now, he could limit his benders to the first week of the month.

Marla, of course, had come to a similar conclusion, which is why she suggested the situation in the first place. She knew how much he loved the inside of a bottle. But most of all, Marla thought of her own taken child (dead now, most likely. Worked to death. *Pale lips. Milky eyes. Red flowers, red flowers, red, red, red*) and thought only of how to protect the Sparrow. Hide the curious curl in her navel and the oddness of her birth, her death and her un-death. Hide everything. She worked twice as hard and sold what she could, and bought fabric for the girl's clothes and leather for her shoes and travelling gear, should they ever need to leave her beloved home at a run, and live out their lives in hiding.

Where would they go? her heart asked her. Marla told her heart to hush.

She hoped that the magic inside the girl—untapped, unknown, unnamed—would remain inside; that if she didn't *know* about the magic, then she would not *use* the magic, and thus no laws would be broken and no unlicensed magic children would be repossessed by the heartless soldiers of the Minister's personal guard.

She would be raised as a regular child—hidden, yes; unconventional in terms of lifestyle, clearly; but fundamentally a *regular child*.

It was a good plan, Marla decided, and it would work. She decided *that*, too.

But then odd things started happening. Things that the girl did not initiate or intend. Instead, it was as though *the magic itself was leaking out*.

The stick that became a snake.

The pebble that became a beetle.

The withered apple tree that, after a single touch, became heavy with apples the size of watermelons.

But surely those could be explained away. The snake was just a trick of the light. The beetle must have been there the whole time, and don't fruit trees always surprise a person—coming back just when you think all is lost? They are the phoenixes of the plant world—though she couldn't quite remember how she knew what a phoenix was. She certainly had never encountered one in a book.

Still, everything was explained, rationalised, forgotten.

For a while.

When the Sparrow turned five, Marla first came to learn that the magic living inside the skin of that child could not always be contained.

It was the first Tuesday of the month. She had sent the junk man packing (he had several bottles rattling around the cart in anticipation of his week-long bender), and had brought the little girl with her to the chicken coops.

Sparrow, then as now, delighted in the populations of multi-coloured birds living in the chicken coop, but saved the majority of her love for a Blue Speckled by the name of Midge—a fat, fine princess of a chicken, with a tall, proud comb atop her head, and two deep red wattles adorning each side of her face like rubies.

Sparrow jumped off the porch in a high, clean arc going much higher and much more slowly than seemed possible; *a trick of the light*, Marla told herself. She landed daintily on the very tips of her toes.

"Well, look at you," Marla said. "A ballerina."

The word stopped her cold.

She had no idea what a ballerina was. She had never seen one, nor had she seen a picture of one, nor had she heard the word before in her life, and yet, there it was; in her mouth, in her memory. *Ballerina*, and not just the word, but the essence of the word as well. In her head was the swell of violins (*what on earth are violins?*), the toes like grace notes on a polished wood floor, the ribbon-wrapped ankles, the long, oiled hair tied back in a hard, round knot. She saw a feathered woman who was both princess and swan, a toy who would be king, a red bird with jewelled eyes (the downfall of tyrants, that bird, and *oh! To have such a bird!*). It was as clear as water, this meaning. As true as the breath in the lungs. *Ballerina. Ballerina. Ballerina.*

The Sparrow looked at Marla and smiled. "Yes," the girl said. "A ballerina. See?" She twirled on one toe, arms extended like wings.

The egg woman felt her heart sink—a heavy stone in a dark, murky pool.

Seeing things I got no right to see; knowing things I never heard of. She shook her head. What other tricks is that girl up to?

When they opened the chicken coop, they saw Midge lying on her side on the packed earth floor, her upper eye muddy and opaque, and gazing at nothing.

"No, no," the child cried. She ran to the far side and skidded to her knees. She paused, held her hands outward as though blessing the bird, great tears streaking down her cheeks and falling onto the chicken's beautiful feathers like rain. She scooped Midge into her arms.

"No, Sparrow," Marla said. "It's too dirty. You'll need another bath, and how many baths can one girl have, really?"

But the girl didn't listen. She buried her face in the stiff breast of the dead hen and couldn't speak for sobbing.

Marla sighed. "There, there, child," she said. "Things live and then they die. There's no use crying over what can't be helped."

The girl wailed louder. She sprang to her feet, clutched her dead chicken and ran from the coop in a rage. The dogs followed her, as always. They never liked to have the child out of their sight.

Marla shook her head. She let the child go. She swept the coop, fed the chickens, fixed the wobbly bits on the fence, and stripped and squatted on the ground to urinate at the four corners as a deterrent for foxes and stoats. When she was finished and re-buttoned, she walked around to the far side of the house and saw the dogs watching the girl as she played with the hen.

The hen.

It was, as before, fat and hale and shining; a princess among hens.

"My Midge," the girl sang. "My Midge, my Midge, my Midge."

The once-dead hen clucked and preened. It was a thing of beauty. It loved the girl, of course it did; everything loved the girl. Marla snatched Sparrow around her waist and hauled her, screaming, inside.

She fed the girl, bathed her and distracted her. She told her stories. She looked out the window to make sure Midge was gone, but Midge wasn't gone, and what's more, there was Midge and an identical Midge strutting through the grass, looking for tasty bugs to catch. Marla closed the curtains and convinced the girl to play in the basement.

By lunch, there were five Midges in the yard. Two of them had laid eggs—fat, speckled and gorgeous, and nestled in the grass. Marla locked the door.

By supper there were fifteen (though there would have been seventeen—a hawk made off with one and another made a fine supper for a passing feral cat).

Marla sighed, and let the girl outside.

"My Midge," the girl sang happily, as she frolicked among the flock of identical chickens. "My Midge, my Midge, my Midge." She kissed each one on each ruby wattle and was, by all reckoning, the happiest girl alive.

Marla sighed. *Fine,* she thought.

That night, Marla told the Sparrow the story of the magic children, and the Boro comet—the source of all this nonsense. She told her how frightened the nation's mothers are each time the Boro comet appears in the sky. She told of the children born with the magic marks, of the soldiers who takes those children away, and of what happens to them.

She told her about the day the junk man found her.

She told her about the Minister. He was old, that Minister, and yet *young*; maintained by magic, hungry for magic. *So hungry.* How he lives alone in that strange fortress stretching up to the sky.

She even told her about her own dear baby; marked, taken. Lost forever.

(*Red flowers, red flowers, red, red, red.*)

The girl listened for a long time, her black eyes sober and serious, a thin slick of tears at the bottom edge.

"Does my junk man know?" the girl asked gravely. "For real, I mean. Does my papa know he is not my papa?" She wrinkled her brow. "It seems like he might not know."

"I know what you mean, love," Marla said. "Your papa lives in a world of his own making. He was there, though, and he knows. But you are wrong in your thinking. It isn't blood what makes a papa a papa. Love does that. Simon's love for you is limitless. Your papa is more papa to you than most can claim." There was a note of bitterness in her mouth. Her own father had turned her out, years ago, when her teenage waist began to swell, and did not welcome her back when the soldiers took her baby away (though he was happy to relieve her of the hefty payment—and she didn't argue. She didn't want it anyway. Blood money, she said). He later died in a brawl, and Marla never mourned him. "Your papa is what he is, and he is doing as fine a job as he can, and he loves you *so very much*. More than you will ever know." For the first time, Marla knew it was true. What's more, she could *feel* it, too.

"Me too," the girl said.

"Not everyone can see you, my darling," Marla said. "But I don't know how long that will last. You are not safe, and you need to be safe. Your papa needs you to be safe." She closed her eyes and closed her fingers around the girl's soft, pliable hands. "*I* need you to be safe."

82

So, as the sun went down, and in the quiet of the loft, surrounded with quilts, candles, safe arms and hushed voices, the girl and her Marla began to make a plan.

The army of Blue Speckled Hens—nearly a hundred of them now—stood guard on the fence, their bright black eyes beading into the night.

21

NOW

THE BUTTERFLY TAKES NOTICE OF THE FLOWERS ALONG THE trail leading to the town, and releases itself from the girl's back in order to gorge itself on pollen.

The dogs whine a bit. They don't like that butterfly; too bright, too big, too unpredictable. They don't like how it clings to the girl, how it refuses to walk on the ground. They whine and growl but they do not snap. The girl lets her fingers linger on their heads, and they calm.

They are *so old*, these dogs, and they love her so much, they feel that they will die without her (which, the junk man daughter knows in her heart, is likely true. *I will miss you*, she thinks).

She reaches the fork in the trail, where one branch goes to town and the other branch wanders up to the top of a rocky knoll. There are seven standing stones at the top of the knoll—remnants, she's heard, of another time, another people, another way of thinking; gone now. No one knows where or why, or when. History is banned, after all. There is only now. There is only the Minister. That is all they ever need know.

The girl smiles. *The Minister.* He has haunted her dreams for as long as she can remember; his damp eyes, his receding hair, the delicate lobes on his ears, fragile and soft between her finger and her thumb. She has not touched the Minister. She has not laid eyes on him, but she knows him, even so. She knows him from the inside out.

She summits the knoll, climbs the tallest of the standing stones and sits, cross-legged, at the top. She cups her hands around her eyes. The Minister's fortress is too far away to see—it is miles and miles and miles away, and yet she can see it all the same; its happenstance form, its blackened windows, its terrible height, its dark stones, each one groaning with the souls of magic children. She can see the Minister too, sitting cross-legged atop his own standing stone, perched on the roof of his impossibly tall tower. Every quarter century, the tower gets taller. Every quarter century, it becomes imbued with more magic. Every quarter century it brings him closer to the thing he desires most of all.

The Boro Comet.

Its strangeness.

Its miracles.

Its curses.

She plucks another hair from her head and weaves it into a pentagram. She then curls her fingers into its centre and pulls, stretching it larger and larger and larger, and as she pulls, the fibres making the pentagram thicken and strengthen. They are rope. They are wire. They are rod-iron. It is a trinket, then a mirror, then a window. She holds it in front of her as though she is hanging a picture on the wall. She jiggles the sides until it feels secure, and lets her hands drift down to her sides. The pentagram floats in front of her, its centre shimmering like the moon on a quiet lake.

She sees him: The Minister, and he sees her. The junk man's daughter. She smiles. He is terrified. She waves. He does not wave back. His mouth opens and closes but nothing comes out. He looks, she thinks, exactly as she imagined him, though his skin is more dull than his billboards lead a person to expect; age, perhaps, or an overindulgence of magic.

Not that she knows anything about magic. She doesn't. How could she?

She stands, slides her arms out of her sleeves, and peels her dress from her shoulders, her chest, her belly. She is before him, naked to the hips, the strange mark on her stomach curling from her navel, glowing so bright to make him squint. There are tears in his eyes.

"You," the Minister says.

"Me," she says. Her eyes glitter. Her teeth flash.

"You're dead."

"Am I?"

"I need you."

"I know." She loves him, so much. She rears back and kicks the pentagram—a quick, sure force. It goes flying away. She can hear him screaming for her to come back, screaming for the guards, screaming for his mother. Screaming, screaming, screaming, and then the pentagram hits the ground, unravels, and his voice is gone.

The dogs wait at the bottom of the standing stone. The butterfly has rested on the head of a Labrador. It is not amused, but it does not fuss at it.

The girl jumps, and lands lightly on her toes. The dogs whine.

"I know," she says. "It's not too much longer."

They head toward town.

22

THEN

IT WASN'T JUST THE CHICKENS. THE CHICKENS WERE JUST THE beginning.

Marla had to build eight new coops to house them all. Fortunately, one of the Midges turned out to be male (she was unsurprised by this—it stood to reason, knowing Midge), and what a male he was. Her entire chicken population—from the Bitter Leafs to the Argonites, to the Peppershells to the Reds—started to wriggle and swoon in his presence. They preened and clucked, and presented their bottoms with a saucy swish. The rooster-Midge only had to turn his head and an entire coop would be sent into a tizzy. Their laying quadrupled overnight. And *what eggs!* They had shimmer and heft. They caused a shiver up the spine at just the touch of them.

Marla came home from her first day in the marketplace selling those eggs with a smile on her face. She bought real beef and shared it with the dogs. She bought a coat for the girl (she told people it was for a country family she knew on hard times). She even bought a new hat for the junk man.

It wasn't until she waved goodbye to the girl and her papa in their handmade cart that she started to worry.

Because *those eggs*.

They did things, those eggs.

Cured illness.

Eased pain.

Repaired marriages.

Within two weeks, six young wives of her acquaintance grew green about the gills, dark circles around the eyes, a glow on the cheeks. They had been trying to get pregnant for several years, and suddenly all six were pregnant at once.

Word got around, but no one said "magic". They didn't dare.

Then there was the herb garden, and the vegetable patch (both, of course, were fed with the manure from the chicken coop—now providing the plants with more than simply nitrogen).

Then it was the cow. Her butter could remove scars, re-grow hair, whiten teeth, and cure arthritis. Her cream cured gout. No one mentioned this—they just bought Marla's wares without making eye contact, and hurried home like the devil was after them.

Marla worried.

Meanwhile, the junk man, with the help of his daughter, was finding more and more curious things in the rubbish heaps; a pair of eyeglasses that allowed the wearer to see in the dark, a pen that never ran out of ink, a picture frame that would show the face of the person that the holder missed most.

The Sparrow helped the junk man to identify these curious objects, and then connect them to the person who needed them most. She had a keen eye for people. She could read them like stories. They didn't see her—not usually, anyway—but she could see them from the inside out, and she loved them.

These objects were few and far between—often they would only find one during the space of a month, and some months would come up empty. Still, as the years passed and as the girl grew, the objects began to proliferate.

Shoes that would allow the wearer to run and run and never tire.

A pot that was always filled with soup.

A blanket that would calm even the fussiest baby.

When the Sparrow was nine, Marla stood in her stall at the Market, selling her eggs by the basketful. She saw the Sparrow and the junk man perched on the cart, selling God-knows-what to God-knows-who.

He saw the church pastor examining a small, leather-bound volume. She saw how his eyes lit up. He stuffed some money in the junk man's hands, tipped his hat to the Sparrow, and hurried away.

The pastor tipped his hat, to the Sparrow. He saw her, noticed her, greeted her. *Not good*, Marla thought. *Not good at all.*

Then a little boy waved at her, and a matron looked the girl up and down, crinkled her nose, gave her a harumph.

Marla sold her last egg, wrapped up a bundle of cookies, and walked across the square.

The Constable sat on a folding chair, under a sign that said TIPS. Under that was a banner that said, "See Lest Ye Be Seen". It was highly produced and shiny, made in the Capitol. The Constable had a sour expression on his face. There was a large glass jar on the rough-hewn table in front of him—the kinds of jar that people use to sour their cabbages in the fall and keep, ripe and stinking, in the corners of their kitchens. But, instead of the slow decay of vegetables, the jar was filled with folded pieces of paper. Anonymous tips. Though, not truly anonymous. Everyone's handwriting was a matter of record. Each note would be collected, smoothed out, and fed into a machine that the Constable had in his office. Failure to provide tips on a regular basis could land a person in the Constable's office—or worse, a visit from the Sedition Squad from the Capitol.

So the tips were collected, and they were largely inane.

The Constable tried not to think about it, and tried to think about fishing instead. The residents of his town—fools, most of them, but they were *his* fools, and that mattered to him—came scurrying over with their paper bits, and went scurrying away without making eye contact. Most of them said things like, *Mrs. Sorenson has a big nose, which means that she's a witch. FYI*, or, *Arlen Riones wrinkled his nose and made a sour expression when the Minister was mentioned*, or, *I would like to divorce my wife, but it is too expensive. Could you just arrest her instead? Yours very truly, Rusty.* They made the Constable's head hurt.

"Hello, Henry," the egg woman said.

The constable started. No one had used his name since he became the constable. He had almost forgotten that he had one to begin with.

"Marla," he said. He gritted his teeth. He remembered the punch. He hoped Marla wasn't still mad at him. "Do you have an observation to share?"

"No, an invitation. There is something that I would like you to see, and something that I feel that you should understand. Can you find your way to my house?"

"I do believe I can." He gazed at the egg woman under the shade of his regulation hat. Her arms were crossed over her ample bosom, and her face was set. Of course he knew where she lived; he also had a history with Marla, and not a happy one. Or, at least the ending wasn't happy. The middle parts were actually rather nice.

"Be there at sundown. Bring a toothbrush."

She walked away.

The constable could have made his way blindfolded.

There was a trick, he had learned, to the constable business; an eye that fluctuated between the blind and the keen, a show of

90

fairness with an open hand toward those who were able to come and go between the Province and the Capitol with ease—factory owners, bureaucrats and the like. He never had to worry about over-expectations—aside from the Inquisitor, none of them lasted very long—and his own gruff presence, which gave the impression of a stricter fist than he actually possessed. There was, he grudgingly allowed, something to be said for maintaining order in a population so weighted by worry, work and weariness that they didn't have time to fool with crime, sedition or independent thinking. The Minister, when it came down to it, knew what he was doing. All hail the Minister.

The constable loved his home, and he hated the Capitol. So he stayed, protected his own (not like he had much choice in the matter; there weren't a lot of retired constables around. They had a tendency to disappear. No one had ever lasted as long as he did. He wasn't going anywhere. He had decided as much).

He arrived at Marla's tiny farm shortly before sunset. The chickens were just settling into their coops, and there were *so many of them*. Hen after hen after identical hen, all murmuring their goodnights to one another. He pulled a cheroot from his pocket and chewed on it thoughtfully. He didn't turn when Marla approached from behind.

"I wouldn't want to have to report an illegal breeding operation, Marla," he said.

"Fortunately, you won't have to," she said.

"Marla, I turn a blind eye to a lot, but this? The Ag Czar is going to—"

"These are not bred birds," Marla said. "They're made."

"What's the difference?"

"They're all the same hen. Midge. They're all Midge."

The constable peered into the coop. The chickens all turned their beaks in unison toward the left. They shivered as one. They blinked as one. He looked carefully from hen to hen, and couldn't find a speck of difference. They weren't just the same breed. They were the *same.*

His mouth went dry. "What are they looking at?"

"I'm getting to that in a minute. First, I want to tell you a story. About a baby."

23

NOW

Jonah kneels in the back yard with his spy scope, gazing up. The ground is damp and the wet soaks deeply into the knees of his trousers. He doesn't care.

The sky is darkening by degrees, but it still isn't dark *enough* for good stargazing. He doesn't care about *that* either. The night, after all, is long. There is plenty of time.

As he waits for the fullness of dark, Jonah enjoys watching the alterations of light—the decay of colour, the way the day strips itself from the surface of the sky. He likes things in *flux*.

There is an object that he hopes to see; a star, perhaps, or a galaxy. It behaves oddly, appearing and disappearing at will. Lately, it has been coming closer and closer to a star known locally as the Eye of Ashra, though it has a different name in different towns—it is his favourite star—approaching, vanishing, approaching, vanishing. He has tracked the odd object's movements. He has documented the quality of its light. He has scratched through equations and theorems. He has an idea; it is too stupid to even write down.

The dew clings to his clothes. He shivers. He has a locket around his neck. His hand grips it absently. Most days, he has forgotten that he has it.

His spyglass is of his own design—a polished wood casing, cast-brass hardware that he poured himself in the hidden work-shop in the barn (this is also where the books are hidden; where they have been hidden for five generations, packed neatly in cedar-lined boxes, taken out only when needed). He harvested the glass himself—usually off the broken glass windows from the munitions factory, though one particularly excellent piece of glass came from a broken-down landship, temporarily abandoned by its soldiers who decided to take an unplanned side-trip to a local tavern (the soldiers were never heard from again, poor things)—and ground them with patience and precision, polishing each piece until it gleamed.

He gives the outer lens a wipe with the chamois in his pocket, clearing off the damp. He positions his face against the eyepiece and waits.

The Sparrow approaches from behind. Her feet are silent on the dampening ground. The dogs and the butterfly are waiting for her in the shadows. They will not come until they are called. They hold watch and do not move.

"Are you real?" Jonah asks. He does not pull away from the eyepiece. He keeps his gaze upon the stars.

The Sparrow says nothing. She is right behind him, so close she can feel the heat from his body, so close she could let her fingers drift in the soft clouds of his breath; so close she could kiss him if she wanted to.

"I think you're real," he says, adjusting the second lens, tipping the whole of the spyglass slightly upward on its hinged tripod.

"How do you know?" the girl whispers.

Jonah yelps in surprise, and scrambles to his feet. He faces the Sparrow, breathing hard. He opens his mouth, closes it, opens it again. He reaches his hand toward her, but thinks better of it, and shoves both hands into the mop of his hair, hanging on tight.

The Sparrow feels her heart in her throat. She smiles. Her body feels more discombobulated than usual, as though each particle in her body is only barely hanging on to one another; as though she may fly apart at any moment. She is hot. She is cold. She shivers all over.

"You're shaking," the boy says. "Are you cold?"

"Yes," she whispers. Her voice wobbles. It is a dry leaf on a windy day. She pinches her face and shakes her head. "No," she corrects herself.

"You are real," the boy says. "Aren't you? You've been real this whole time."

She says nothing. Her skin is heat and light, sweat and goose-bumps. Her face is tight with hope.

He stands, brushes the grass and damp from his knees. There will be no moon tonight. The sky will be so dark it will hurt to look at it. The stars will stab the eye. The girl is beautiful in the fading light. She is the most beautiful thing he has ever seen. Her skin glows orange and pink, and damp grey. She is an opal in the gloom. He is dizzy. He wants to touch her but he doesn't.

He has seen her before. He has talked to her before—and she to him. He remembers it now, standing in front of her. He remembers it all. He remembers that each time he sees her, he has a similar flood of remembering—that each meeting vanishes when she vanishes, and unfolds again before him when she returns; that her presence opens his mind like a map, and when she leaves it flutters away, as though snatched by a strong wind.

He knows that the last time he saw her, he nearly kissed her.

Nearly.

"Will I forget you this time?" he asks, a sob hiding in his throat. He feels a needle in his heart, and he sees her wince.

Is it the same needle? he wonders. *Is it the same thread, pulling at my heart and her heart?* He does not say it out loud. She takes a step closer.

"I don't know," she says. There is too much breath in her voice, as though she is already fading. He reaches out his hand, palm up; an invitation. She accepts, lays her palm on his, as light and hot as ash. He nearly blisters from the heat of it.

"Are you sick?" he asks.

"I am," she says. "But not for long. Soon I will never be sick again—but I need you to help me."

"What can I do?" His breath comes in quick, short gasps, his soul escaping in sigh after sigh after sigh. He doesn't blink, he doesn't want to miss her for a second. With everything in him, he tries to stitch her in place in his mind.

"Leave a note for your mother. Tell her you'll be back when everything changes, and tell her to cover for you."

The Sparrow waits for a long time in the growing dark. She lays her hand on the homemade spyglass. She knows that Jonah had a brother, two years younger than he, who was taken away by soldiers on the day that she had been left on the trash heap. She knows that his family does not talk about the lost boy—worked away to nothing by now. The Sparrow has no idea what happened to the children like her—not *really*—but she has always suspected the worst. Even in her situation, her life-long attempts to suppress the magic welling up inside her, she knows she can't last long; already, she can feel her body yearning to disassemble, fly apart, scatter across the landscape like mist. It doesn't frighten her, this thought of her own dissolution. She only wants to make it *matter*.

All this magic, pulled up by the comet. It's too much for one person. *Spread it around*, she thinks. *Bless the land and the people on it.*

The minutes tick by. The wind picks up. The stars keep their rigid courses in the dark sky. She crouches down and hangs onto her knees with her jacketed arms.

"Come," she calls, and the dogs and the butterfly come. The dogs take posts on either side of her, while the butterfly alights on her back.

The boy comes, too, carrying food in a satchel. He has been well brought up; his parents have taught him to plan for the future, to provide for himself and others. They have raised him to be a good person—and he is.

The Sparrow stands. The dogs growl. The boy hands her a bit of homemade bread and honey. She eats it gratefully.

"Where are we going?" he asks, and she knows he will follow her anywhere.

"We are going to meet the Minister," she says, with her mouth full. "But we don't have to go far. He will be coming to us."

24

THEN

THE DAY AFTER MARLA TOLD HIM ABOUT THE BABY—NOT A
baby anymore, really, now a girl—the Constable put a sign on the
door of his office, *The Constable Is Ill Today. Please Refrain From
Committing Crimes Until Tomorrow.*

It was not the first time he used that sign—indeed, it was heavily
wrinkled and ragged around the edges, rain-blotched, and oddly
effective. Every time he had actually *been* out ill, the town residents
who might normally bend toward rule breaking followed the sign
to the letter. Bar fights ceased, petty thievery vanished, employee
insubordination all but evaporated, and domestic disturbances were
blissfully unavailable.

There were times when the Constable put the sign up just to give
everyone a break from themselves.

On this day, though, he locked himself in the back room of the
Constable's Office—the room with no windows, one door and one
lock to which he had the only key—and did not come out, no matter
how hard the egg woman knocked.

He had a jug of Special Occasion Whiskey, one that he received as a gift from his mother the day he was appointed to his position (a bald-faced attempt at brown-nosing, the constable knew, but he appreciated it all the same). He'd never touched it in all those years, but he would do so now.

That baby.

He took out his notes and files—illegal, probably—on the birth of the stillborn magic child, of its mother's eventual unravelling, of its days in the box on his desk, of the sounds (oh, God, that laughing) that came from…*somewhere*. He couldn't say where. Indeed, he did not want to.

Whiskey, in the end, tastes no better in the dark than in the light, and it certainly is not improved with lack of sleep or a hot, morning mouth, or a belly raging for some kind of food.

*He threw that child on the rubbish heap. A baby, for God's sake, and by some miracle…*He shook his head. He couldn't even *think* it.

The cardboard box haunted his dreams.

The sound of a laughing baby, from that day to this, *any* baby, made him shiver and quake.

He hated the Minister. *Hated* him.

The egg woman gave him three days to think—or in this case, *drink*—on it before she came in with her tools and her grim silence.

Working quickly, she removed the door from the wall, hoisted up the mostly-unconscious constable onto her shoulders, and heaved him into the back alley, where she could wet him efficiently with the cistern hose. He stood there under the back awning, dripping and cold, his nose and eyes running with old rainwater, old regrets and new sorrow. He let out one, long, lonely wail, and let it die in his throat. He closed his mouth and shivered in silence.

Marla let the hose fall to the ground. "Are you quite through?" she said.

The constable nodded.

She offered a curt, grim nod in return. "Very good. Now, if you wouldn't mind putting on dry clothes and following me, there are things that I would like to discuss, and it wouldn't do to have such conversations on government property."

The constable did as he was told. He made a stop at the shower, cleaned the stink of the last few days on his skin and slid into clean clothes. He slumped his shoulders and bowed his head and went outside next to the egg woman, and allowed her to lead him.

The junk man and the girl were camped on a small hillock just outside of camp. It was one of their favourite spots. Three of the Midges had escaped the coop and were hunting for bugs in the grass, and the girl sat in the branches of one of the trees, encouraging a nest full of baby birds to crawl onto her dress, as the mama bird looked on indulgently.

The junk man squatted by the fire, roasting fat, greasy sausages on sticks.

"I hope you're hungry, my bird," he called up to the girl in the tree.

"Simon," Marla said sharply.

The junk man looked up and nearly fell onto the ground. "TRAITOR," he shouted.

"I am no such thing. I have brought us an ally. Sit."

The girl listened as the three adults discussed her future. They said things like *escape plans* and *protective custody* and *worst-case-scenario*. She could hear their worry and their fear. She could hear the echoes of loss.

They spoke of the Minister. Their voices trembled with fear, and hatred.

"He can't have her," the junk man said, his voice was dangerous— the rusty edge of an old tin can. "I'd die first."

"Yup," the constable said, rubbing his face. "She does seem to have that effect. Did when she was a baby, too, or a dead baby. In any case,

I pretty much feel the same way. The Minister takes too much, and enough is enough."

The girl listened intently. The mother bird flew away to find food, and the babies had been replaced in the nest. They cried out—not for their mother, but for the junk man's daughter. She frowned.

She didn't understand everything that the adults said. She did not fear as they feared; she did not hate as they hated, but she knew this: she had something inside her. Something special, and a bad man wanted it (or a good man; or a bad man who could change; a human being deserving of love, and *oh, how she loved*. How she loved everyone).

She looked up at the sky. The sun hovered over the horizon, fat and bright and lurid; a delight of colour, and it was for everyone. It shone equally on Minister and junk man, on soldier and egg woman, on dogs and hens and bugs. It cannot be claimed by a single individual—it shines for all.

Well, she thought, *what if I did what the sun does? What if he came and the magic was gone? What if I gave it to everyone else instead?*

As she drifted to sleep, she dreamed of a wave, swelling up beneath her feet. She smelled foam, wind and salt. Yellow coins, red flowers, a child that lived. A particularly fine hen. She was speed, pull and tide. She felt herself lift, bubble, dissolve. She felt the wave cover the world.

And she disappeared.

25

NOW

IN THE END, IT DOES NOT MATTER THAT THE INQUISITOR DID NOT make the customary stop in the baker's shop, and that he did not purchase a pie for his wife (one that, surely, would have saved his marriage, cured his gout, straightened his back, ended his impotence, ensured his raise, and set his career on a more prosperous track. The benefits of pie are well-known and numerous—the apples, after all, came from Marla's farm).

Despite the dark that night, despite the jittering fear choking the town every time someone from the Capitol comes calling, every window along that dark street peeked through drawn curtains and watched that black car as it slid to the Constable's office. They held their breath as it slid away.

The Inquisitor, people whispered. *Here?* They wondered and fussed, but they did not look up. They shut their curtains and counted their children, and looked around their houses for anything incriminating.

Now, days later, they continue to whisper. They continue to fuss. They confer, collect and collude. A crowd forms in the square.

They speak of nothing else. Inquisitors, it is determined, don't just visit towns for their health, and the Minister's eye doesn't stray on communities by accident.

That thing that no one talks about.

That thing that no one *says*.

Well, someone blabbed.

But who? Who is the blabbermouth? The Mayor? Surely not. Not the constable, neither; Constable's got everyone's back—that's well known. Maybe the tax collector? Or the orphan matron, or the junk man.

Yes, the preacher nods, the junk man. That's who told. Must have been.

"Heard it from his own lips," the preacher says. "Junk man told me just before he sold me this here watch. I mean bible."

He clears his throat, gives his fist a quick shake and the gold watch in his palm vanishes. In its place is a bible—dusty, well-worn, lovingly thumbed. The preacher smiles. If he decides to shake it again, it will become a glass tumbler of good whiskey, served neat. Beautiful thing. God bless the junk man. Despite the unpleasant aroma, the gentleman knows his business, that's for sure—links the right product to the right man, always, and this little beauty, thinks the preacher, is the rightest of them all. He licks his lips and grips his bible tight. *Soon,* he tells himself. Once he has left his insufferable flock for a blessed minute alone.

He gazes out at his community with what he hopes is a beatific and forgiving expression. "But the junk man only reports rumours, and does not participate in vice. Remember this, my friends. Let us not judge—"

"Nah," a neighbour interrupts, "the junk man never knows nothin'. It was the egg woman. The egg woman knew it first. Heard it from her last week, and that's a fact."

"You never did," Marla, the egg woman, says. She had been

standing in the shadows, listening. How strange that no one noticed her. *Very strange.* She gives the man a swat on the backside of his head. The man rubs the injury, mutters something that sounds like, *didn't see you there,* and stares at the ground. Marla gives him a hard look. She is also agitated, some notice. She scans the crowd, and beyond them. She searches the sky; she is looking for something.

"I only heard it just now. Just like you." She says it like she means it.

It's true enough. They all know *just now.* That's why they're talking in the first place. But who knew *first?* Well, this is important. Lives might be at stake, and the crowd is divided.

"The schoolteacher," says another neighbour. "Must'a'been. She has that look on her."

"Or the men at the Soldiers' Home."

"I think it was the undertaker."

"No, the butcher. Pretty sure."

"Or the washer women."

"Or the miller."

"Or the miller's shiftless sons."

"The children told me," says another. "It is always the children who know."

"By the way, has anyone seen my son? He left before we woke."

Everyone's children left before dawn. School project, their notes said. Odd, but no matter. There are more important things to be dealt with; not getting arrested, for starters.

The town murmurs and frets. They practice their excuses and alibis until they know them by heart. They imagine what they will say to the constables, or the soldiers, or the Inquisitors. They pick at their teeth, rub at their beards and shoot worried glances at the road.

An unlicensed magician, people whisper. *Here, Of all places.* They shake their heads, carefully layering incredulity into their voices. *Well. My stars.*

Marla, the egg woman, listens to the conversation for as long as she can tolerate. She lives, she knows, in a village of idiots situated at the edge of a nation of morons. There are worse things, of course.

Though, in truth, not many.

She clutches her basket as though it is a raft in a stormy sea. The basket is light—today she sold nearly all of her eggs. It didn't seem to soothe her. Her eagle gaze pierced windows and alleys, made sweeps under carts and benches; she was desperate. She rubs her hands until they are raw.

No one knew for sure, of course, what a magician looked like—unlicensed or not. Who had met a magician, after all? One that wasn't a baby, that is? The only thing for sure was that magic belonged to the government, which is to say that it was given, freely and forever, to the Beloved Minister, and him alone. The unlicensed practice of magic? Well, there were punishments for that sort of thing.

Harsh punishments.

No one knew what those were, and indeed the idea that anyone could even attempt at magic was a bit of a head-scratcher; it's not like there are any books on the subject, or stories. Magic is a banned subject, after all.

Clearly, the town decides, they are all blameless. One by one, they excuse themselves. One by one, they hurry home. They whistle as they locked up their apple-producing bowls, their bottomless liquor bottles and their baby-soothing blankets.

Marla the egg woman sits on the stone edge of the fountain. She presses her basket to her ample bosom, and waits.

By noon, the junk man arrives. He sits next to her. He hesitates, swallows nervously, then lets his bony arm drape across her shoulders. She doesn't shrug him away. Their eyes are red. Their noses are red. Their cheeks are the colour of ash.

At mid-afternoon, the constable sits down as well. He feels he should offer them something. He has nothing to give.

"Where is our child?" the egg woman asks.

"What has she done?" the junk man sighs.

They do not move from that spot. By late afternoon, the first landship arrives, and another, and another. They encircle the town, like a noose.

26

NOW

THOUGH THE SECRECY WEIGHS HEAVILY ON HER CONSCIENCE, THE junk man's daughter knows it is for the best. Her papa and her Marla could not be permitted to know. They'd only try to stop her.

And it is too late for that.

As the landships arrive, the Sparrow and Jonah race down the quiet alleys. They have no intention of going to sleep— not for a moment. They spend every second of the night together, going from house to house, holding tightly to one another's hands as they run through the town. They rap on windows. They cry through the locks.

They are looking for children, asleep in their beds.

"Come," they whisper. "Come with us." And they come, as young as five and as old as twenty. They rub the sleep from their eyes, and throw homemade woollens over their nightclothes. They tramp silently into the dewy starlight.

"Okay," the children whisper. "We'll come. We'll follow you anywhere."

They can see the Sparrow. They cannot imagine a world where

they can *not* see the Sparrow They love her, as she loves them. *So much.*

The butterfly clings to the Sparrow's back, making her look as though she had luminescent wings—which is helpful, because it makes it easier to see in the dark. The dogs lope along the sides of the growing crowd, herding the stragglers back to the group.

"This way," the Sparrow calls, "to the rubbish heap. It's where things start."

None of the children had ever been to the rubbish heap—indeed, they were warned away from it; there were rumours that it was haunted by ghosts, and if not ghosts, the junk man, who was just as bad—the way he talks to himself, the way he has conversations with people who are not there.

"Trust me," the Sparrow says. And they do. They trust her implicitly

Jonah refuses to let go of her hand, even though his hand is blistered and raw. It has begun to ooze. He won't be able to use that hand for a month, he figures, but it is worth it. He'd rather cut his hand off than let go of the girl with the butterfly wings. He will hang onto her, until he can't.

The Sparrow is barely there. She can feel each cell, each molecule, each electron cloud. She can feel the bonds between every speck begin to shiver and moan. She is a thing in flux; not particle, not wave. Something else.

"The Boro comet," she tells the children, "does not cause the magic. I was born under the comet's influence, but it is not the comet that made me what I am. There is an ocean underground—an ocean that, even now, is beginning to swell. There is a tsunami under our feet, and we are going to ride it."

The children don't know what surfing is. They don't know how to catch a swell and ride it into shore.

But they do. They have, as one, an image of a brown girl wearing very little, moving like a snake over a foamy wave. They hear every song, they see every movie, they read every book. In an instant, they see everything; images of the world as it was.

Fascinating, the children think.

"I don't know what it will look like, all this magic covering the world. I don't know what it will do. I do know that forcing that much power through that few people is dangerous. It drains the life right out of them. The other magic children are dead. They died a long time ago. I am the only one left."

"But the Minister—"

"If we are all blessed, then we are all empowered. If we are all enhanced, then we are all protected, and if the magic is diluted, then there will be nothing for the Minister to mine."

"How will it happen?"

"It is already happening. You felt it, didn't you?"

They do. They had been feeling it for days; the buzz in their ankle bones, the crackle in the air, the slightly wobbly feeling, as though the ground under their feet was about to give way.

"Hold hands," the Sparrow says. "The first wave is about to hit."

27

NOW

SOLDIERS FLANK THE LANDSHIPS, AND MOVE IN PROCESSION INTO the town, marching by twos along the West Road, their faces hidden behind the perpetual grins of their metal masks, the required iron rings welded around their throats.

Once a soldier, always a soldier, whisper the townspeople as they pass. *Poor things.*

The soldiers' boots are polished to a high gleam. Each smart stride leaves the smile of their heels pressed into the ooze of the road. Their knees snap smart; their wool-clad thighs whip forward with certainty and aggression; their electric eyes do not drift to the right or the left, their progress more sure than an arrow's shot.

The junk man hails them as they pass.

"Welcome misters," he says, with a toothless grin as they march by. The egg woman elbows him in the ribs. Her hair stands on end. Her eyelashes have begun to singe. It isn't just nervousness that makes her feel this way; there is something coming. It is underground. It is in the air. It is all around them.

28

NOW

THE CHILDREN HEAD INTO TOWN AT A RUN. THEY ARE SUN, water and wave; kinetic energy. They are comet, star and nebulae; the vacuum of space, the multi-layered folds of time. They are all these things at once, and they are *beautiful*.

Frogs appear in their pockets. Birds appear overhead. They have cat's ears or lizard's tails or wings. They are in flux. They are giants, then elves, then nothing at all. Another wave hits. They change again.

The butterfly clings to the Sparrow's back, lifting her above the crowd. Jonah runs below her, keeping the girl in view. His hand is burned. It will scar. He does not care.

The Sparrow sees the landships surrounding the town. She sees the soldiers crowding the streets. She laughs.

"That's not a landship," she says. The children below her agree.

"It's a bunny," one of the smaller children says, and indeed, the landship *is* a bunny. It was always a bunny. It has a bow around its neck. It is a gift.

"And that one is a cow," another child says, pointing at the next landship.

"And that one is an ice-cream cart."

"And that one is my mom."

As landship after landship transforms, their occupants go tumbling out onto the ground. Soldiers. They are flabbergasted.

The Sparrow blows a kiss at a soldier. His mask transforms into a butterfly and flutters away. His eyes—now simply flesh—flood with tears. He falls to his knees.

"An angel," he cries, as another soldier is freed.

"A god," cries the next.

The children run faster as the swell of earth moving behind them increases speed. There is now an opening, and they leave the rest of the landships as they are.

"The fountain," the Sparrow calls. "Run to the fountain."

The Minister is waiting for them. His personal landship has parked in the centre of the square. It is deserted, save for a bone-thin man, a boulder-thick woman and a man in a constable's uniform, sitting side by side on the fountain wall.

The Minister looks down. They stare blankly back.

Imbeciles, he thinks. *They must be imbeciles.*

He can feel the magic in the air. He can taste it on his tongue. He thinks of his tower—his beautiful tower. He thinks of the Boro comet, due to come in a decade. What's a decade to a man so enhanced? It is like waiting for afternoon tea. He imagines grasping the comet in his hands. He imagines devouring its magic, crunching it between his molars. He imagines becoming sated, at last.

He thinks of his mother's face. That scar curving down her cheek. He thinks of her polished boots, marching away. Magic can bring her back. He is sure of it. If only he can catch that comet, just as she told him to, all those years ago.

He hears the sound of small feet. He hears the voices of children. He feels their breathing and their energy and their joy.

Red flowers, he thinks. *Red, red, red, red.*

The Minister presses his hands to his mouth. He falls to his knees.

He wishes he had earplugs to cover up his screams.

29

NOW

THE SPARROW SEES THE MINISTER ON THE DECK OF A LANDSHIP, weeping like a child. He shivers and shakes. He rests his head on his knees. He calls for his mother.

"Oh," she says, her voice echoing strangely on every surface of the town. She is a chorus, a flock of sparrows flying away. "You poor, poor man."

The Minister looks up. He is so afraid. Still he stands. Still he tries to look the part.

"My wayward magician," he calls out. His voice squeaks. He is both enraged and embarrassed. "At last."

The Sparrow floats above him. It is not the butterfly's doing anymore. The children crowd into the square. They are a chattering mass, surrounding the landship and the fountain. They climb trees, balance on signs and climb on top of carts.

The Sparrow glances down at the junk man and the egg woman, still sitting on the edge of the fountain.

"My baby," the junk man says.

"My baby," the egg woman whispers.

It's true. She is their child, the both of them. The constable is her grandfather. Of course he is. How sorry she will be to leave them. Even now, she is not solid. She is a storm cloud, an electric shock. She will strike, and then she will dissipate. This is the way of things.

"I have come to give you a present," the Sparrow says.

"I am here to receive it," the Minister seethes. His voice is syrup, it is oil. It leaves a slick on the skin that does not wash off.

There is another wave coming, the largest yet. The Sparrow is unstable. She could blow at any minute. She turns to her mother and her father and her grandfather. She looks at Jonah. Her heart shivers and breaks.

"I love you," she says. "I love you, I love you, I love you. Don't forget me."

The wave surges under the junk heap (strange animals made of old boots, broken glass and springs scatter into the forest), under the munitions factory (each bullet becomes a blossom, each firearm a shovel, each chemical a love note to the broken-hearted), and under the school (the chalk grows arms and legs, the switch grows wings, each desk becomes a hammock and the floor grows flowers).

The Sparrow lands before the Minister. She holds out her hand. He lays his own upon it, palm to palm. It burns. He winces.

"Are you sick?"

"Yes," she says. "But not for long."

The wave arrives. It surges under the fountain and pours out the top. It submerges the town, submerges the farms, submerges the forests and the roads, and the other sectors. The Capitol. The magic pours and pours and pours.

"What are you doing?" the Minister whispers.

"An act of love," the Sparrow whispers back, and she kisses him on the mouth.

There is heat. There is light. There is a crack in the world. There is the sound of something exploding—or something coming together. The Minister cannot tell.

The Minister sees his mother. He sees stars. He sees the Boro comet, hanging like a jewel around his own neck. He wraps his fingers around it. He traces his finger along the scar on his mother's face, like a meteor streaking across the sky.

"I knew it," he said.

Then there is only darkness.

The Minister is gone.

30

NOW

It has been thirty-seven days, and the junk man has not found his cart. There are reports that it has grown a stag's head, and has been seen in the forest, happily munching the bark off a young maple tree.

The junk man isn't sure how he feels about this. He is fairly certain that the cart itself is made from maple. Wouldn't that be cannibalism? He isn't sure, but he is worried about his cart's current moral path.

He hasn't had a drink in over a month. He is suddenly very worried about moral paths.

He sees to the farm while Marla is indisposed. She hasn't gotten out of bed since...

People called it *The Blessing*, and maybe it was. The soldiers were freed, after all. The Minister disappeared in a flash of light, and the strange things that had been leaking from the girl all those years...well, they are everywhere. The world is now filled with sparrows. He grimaces just thinking about it. He swallows acid into his gut.

My Sparrow, my Sparrow, my Sparrow. Each heartbeat is an elegy.

He feeds the chickens by hand. The red plumes, the purple bantams, the snow-white silkies, and of course, the legions of Midges. The Midges take the longest—primarily, because there are so many, but they also have been refusing to eat. They miss the girl. Everyone misses the girl, even those who never laid eyes on her in their lives. They weep and mourn and rend their hair. They are desolate. The junk man croons and cajoles, and finally persuades each Midge to eat. They do so begrudgingly. They remember how the girl loved him. They are doing it for the Sparrow.

The junk man goes inside, his egg basket now quite full. He has also gathered tomatoes, herbs and a dark purple pepper. He whips the eggs, fries the vegetables, and makes an omelette. He has never made an omelette. He has never even had one. He has never known the word *omelette* until this moment, but there it is—fluffy and delicate and perfect; a delight to the tongue.

So many things he can do now. He tells himself it is because he has given up the bottle. He knows it is because of the wave.

"Here," he says, entering Marla's room and throwing open the curtains. "Eat." He sets the tray on the bedside table. He even included a vase of flowers.

"Go away," the egg woman says. "I hate you."

"I know," the junk man says. "But I will not go away. You're all I have left, and I love you. Hell, I've loved you for most of my life."

He rests his hand on hers. They do not move. They stay that way, their grief pressing on their chests, for a long, long time. Very slowly, she allows her fingers to interlace with his. Very slowly, she hooks him close, and hangs on tight.

31

THEN

THE NIGHT MARLA BROUGHT THE CONSTABLE TO THEIR CAMP, the Sparrow woke up while everyone else was still asleep.

The fire was low. The junk man had laid out blankets for the egg woman and the constable and himself, and they curved toward its fading heat.

The Sparrow stared at the fire for a long time, until the logs blazed and a pile of glowing coals piled in the centre. She watched as the bodies of the adults unravelled a bit, and relaxed. They would sleep longer if they were warm. She climbed out of her tree and ran down the darkened trail.

The Tice house slept hard in the dark. Though the Vox's harsh rattle woke other families, the Tices' chose to keep their pillows unpatriotically over their ears. They slept through it. They didn't even stir.

"REMEMBER CITIZENS," the Vox concluded as she slid open the window, "NO ACT OF LOVE FOR OUR BELOVED MINISTER IS TOO SMALL. HE LOVES YOU. HE LOVES EVERY ONE OF YOU. WHAT WILL YOU DO TO SHOW YOUR LOVE TO OUR DEAR LEADER?"

The Sparrow stood in the living room. What *would* she do? She had an idea. She imagined the wave. She imagined it moving through her, moving through whatever she touched. *He loves magic,* she thought. *He loves it so much, and he could be a part of it forever. Dissolved, unified. A blessing.*

He would never have enough. Not the way he was going after it. This was the only way to make him happy.

She tiptoed up the stairs, and climbed into Jonah Tice's bed.

"Wake up," she said, cuddling close.

He smiled.

"It's you."

"It's me."

"I remember you, and then you go away, and then I don't remember you. How do you do that?"

"I don't know." The thought of it made her incredibly sad.

"I'm glad you're here now," he said, and he held her hand.

"Do you have a pocket knife?

He did. The Sparrow unwound one of her braids. She pulled out a lock of hair and cut it with the knife, tying it into a tight bow and fitting it inside a locket that she had found on the rubbish heap just the other day. She put it around Jonah's neck and secured the clasp.

"Isn't this for a girl?" he asked.

"No, it's for me to give to you, and for you to keep. One day, I will disappear. Either you will remember me, or you won't."

"I'll remember you."

"Sometimes you don't."

Jonah hung his head. It was true, and it shamed him. He imagined a needle and thread, stitching the memory of her into his soul. He felt himself bleed. He gripped the pendant. "I'll never take it off. Never."

"See that you don't. When I disappear, throw the locket into the fountain."

"And then what?"

"Maybe I'll come back. Or maybe you'll remember me, and that will be enough."

"That's not enough."

"It's enough for me. Promise. Promise you will."

"Don't go."

"*Promise.*"

He listened to the snore of his parents, the song of crickets, the lonely cry of an owl in the dark. He hugged the Sparrow, who hugged him back.

"I promise."

They fell asleep with their arms wrapped around one another, hanging on for dear life.

When Jonah woke, the Sparrow was gone. He didn't remember her at all.

32

NOW

Jonah doesn't keep his promise at first. The blast from the magic wave sent him flying backwards. He hit a street lamp, cracking his skull. The egg woman carried him in her arms to the doctor, who wasn't sure he would make it.

Indeed, he didn't want to make it. He watched the Sparrow disappear in a burst of light. There was nothing left of her. His heart would never heal.

Unfortunately, while his heart did not heal, his skull and his brain *did*, and when he woke, his pendant was gone.

Gone.

No one remembered seeing it.

His mother gathered him home to finish his recuperation. He refused to go out. He refused to eat. He stayed indoors for months, drawing pictures of the night sky and throwing them into the fire to be burned.

Finally, six months after the wave, Jonah wakes in the middle of the night. He hears a voice calling his name. He tiptoes downstairs, and sees that the bowl of flowers in the centre of the hand-planked table are gone. In its place is a locket. His locket.

He opens it up and sees the knot of hair. He brings it to his lips. It gives him a shock, like electricity. Grabbing his coat and slipping on his boots, he runs into the night.

There is no moon, and the stars are sharp and cold, each one a bright pin holding up the sky. They are so beautiful, his heart begins to break.

No, he thinks, *it is already broken.*

He presses the knot of hair against his sternum. Unaccountably, his heart feels more whole than it ever has. He feels as though he is floating, and who knows? He may well be. The world is changing, after all.

The town sleeps. No one is out. No one but Jonah.

There is a statue of the Sparrow next to the fountain. She is holding a Most Remarkable Hen. There is a very large butterfly on her back. Her hair billows behind her like a storm. Red flowers grow at her feet. It is the first time he has seen it, and he nearly collapses in grief. He hardly knew her. He loves her anyway.

Throw it in the fountain. That's what she said.

And then what? is what he asked.

He doesn't stop to wonder now. He throws the locket and the knot of hair into the fountain—a great, wild hope surging in his chest, like a wave.

"I remember you," he whispers. "I remember and remember and remember. Now and forever, I remember you."

He closes his eyes and waits.